DEATH UNDER HYPNOSIS

BOOK 12 IN THE DI GILES SERIES

ANNA-MARIE MORGAN

ALSO BY ANNA-MARIE MORGAN

In the DI Giles Series:

For Caroline, with love

1

A MURDER REMEMBERED

June 1990.
Sheila.

The forest smelled of earth and fresh growth. Every green, vibrant and vivid.

Her ears filled with birdsong and the incessant knocking of a woodpecker, hunting crawlies somewhere in the distance.

Her skin prickled, nerves tingling as she filled her lungs with the early summer air. What a day to be alive.

The sun, breaking through the canopy, created shards of light like a luminous curtain. It looked touchable, as though she might scoop it up or push it to the side to see what lay beyond.

Everything was brilliant light or life-filled shade. Her feet bounced on the moss-covered ground. Sheila looked down at them, her eyes pausing on the axe she held in both hands. Heavy. Sharp. Deadly.

Then the hut. A wooden shack. A broken, bleeding edifice in need of care and paint.

The smile left her face, replaced by something ugly.

She used the axe to smash open the door, sick with rage and hatred. Glaring at the entity inside. She must destroy the evil. There would be no other way.

As she saw the dirty, tear-stained woman, Sheila knew what she had to do. Annihilate her.

The axe became lightweight with adrenaline as she raised it above her head, bringing it down like she would chop logs for the fire.

The woman cried out, begging for her life, pulling at the chains holding to the floor.

Sheila brought the weapon down, closing her eyes against the face. Again. And again. Obliterating the entity, forever.

∼

Jane Doe.

SHE TUGGED *at the chain attaching her to the structure. Nothing gave, save for her throbbing wrists, which burned as though dipped in flaming sulphur.*

Each twist cut her a little more. They had sharpened the cuffs. She could see the score marks left by a file. Someone had gone to a lot of trouble.

Trying to remember how she had ended up in this hell, she leaned back, closing her eyes.

She had been heading to the newsagents for a paper and milk. Behind her, the engine of a car. She turned.

The car, what colour was it? What make was it? She couldn't remember. The image was shrouded in mist. A hand reached out to her. What else? She strained her mind. Why was it so difficult to recall?

She prostrated herself and sobbed.

SHE MUST HAVE FALLEN ASLEEP. How long for, she wasn't sure. Just as she wasn't sure how long they had holed her up in this hell. How many times had night fallen? Four? Five? Why was she sleeping so much? And why did her left arm ache below the shoulder?

Puncture marks? Bruises and tiny wounds marred her upper arm. Thinking hurt. Moments came and went. Little made sense.

The door bust open. The shock set her body shaking, her chains rattled, vibrating against the makeshift wooden floor.

She saw rage and violence in that face. It was like nothing she had ever witnessed.

The weapon raised.

"No... Please, don't-"

When the first blow landed, she lost all consciousness. That was the only blessing as carnage followed.

THE BEGINNING

The morning was crisp and clear, with a piercing sunlight, in contrast to the damp mist of the previous night. Hoar frost covered the trees, grass and shrubs. Frozen leaves crunched under her feet.

Yvonne took the car keys from her pocket, the car beeping expectantly.

The DI and Tasha were the last to leave Aberystwyth police station, as Yvonne had returned that morning to finish the last of the paperwork.

Tasha needed the ladies' room before the drive back to Newtown. She left the DI to amble, deep in thought, to the car.

Across the road from Yvonne, a middle-aged woman pushed her sunglasses up onto her head and peered at her.

The DI cast a glance behind, to see if the woman was looking at someone else. She wasn't.

"Are you okay?" she asked as the woman approached. She noted the long, greying hair held back in a ponytail. The woman had her hands pushed deep inside the pockets of her long, woollen coat.

"Are you DI Giles? DI Yvonne Giles?"

Yvonne squinted in the bright sunlight. "Yes, I am."

"My name is Sheila Winters."

"What can I do for you?" The DI's gut tightened uncomfortably. It was something about the other-worldliness of the woman's stare. It disconcerted her. Like the woman was looking, but not seeing. She was viewing through and beyond as though experiencing another time and place.

"I've heard you are one of the best at solving cases and finding murderers." The woman stopped just in front of Yvonne, blocking her path.

Behind her, the DI could hear the door of the station opening and closing. Thank God Tasha was coming. "I don't know about being the best Mrs Winters but, yes, I have caught a few murderers in my time. What's wrong? Do you need help?"

The woman nodded. Her face appeared gaunt and haunting, half-shadowed as it was by the morning sun.

"Mrs Winters?" Yvonne asked again, as the woman continued with her thousand-yard stare.

"Is everything all right?" Tasha was at the DI's shoulder.

Yvonne shrugged. "I don't know." She tilted her head to peer at the lady. "Mrs Winters?" she said with increased volume.

The woman jumped. "Yes, Sorry."

"You meant to say something?" Yvonne frowned, confused by what was going on with the woman. "Has there been a murder?"

"Yes, I think so."

The DI scratched her head. "You think?"

"Sorry, I know I'm not making much sense."

"What's happened?" Yvonne asked with greater urgency. She wanted to give Sheila Winters a shake. She didn't.

"I think I murdered someone." Sheila turned piercing blue eyes to her. There was intelligence in those eyes. And pain. "I think I murdered someone thirty years ago, when I was twenty years old. I killed another young woman. I don't know who, I don't know where, and I don't know why…"

"You'd better come inside." Yvonne motioned Mrs Winters towards the station.

Sheila nodded and made her way to the door.

"Would you like me to stay?" Tasha asked, her face lined with concern and the quiet discomfort the woman's spaced-out demeanour caused her.

Yvonne squeezed Tasha's hand. "Thank you," she whispered as she turned to follow Sheila Winters.

The DI took her to an interview room. "Please, take a seat, Mrs Winters." She grabbed a pen. "Now, let's go back to the beginning. Why do you think you murdered someone?"

Sheila deposited her small frame onto the chair. Her hands shook as she straightened her skirt. "I feel foolish," she said, her eyes glistening as she fixed them on the corner of the room.

Yvonne could tell Sheila was not seeing the interview room at all, preoccupied by this other place in her mind. "Don't feel foolish. Begin when you are ready."

"I see it." The words shot forth. Staccato.

"See what?"

"The blood."

"Whose blood?"

Sheila shook her head. "I don't know. It's everywhere, thick and sticky."

"On you?"

"Yes, on my hands, my clothes, the floor, and on the walls."

"You said this occurred thirty years ago?" Yvonne leaned in.

"Yes." Sheila nodded. "Yes, I think so."

"You think?"

"I know it's a long time ago. I was having treatment. I'd forgotten. I'd forgotten everything until two weeks ago."

"I meant to ask why you waited until now to come forward, but you are telling me that you have only recently remembered?"

"Yes, only now." Mrs Winters' eyes glazed over. Her words came in slow, hushed tones.

"So, What you saying, is that you are having dissociated recall and flashbacks, like a sort of PTSD?"

"I see scenes and hear words. I see dimly lit rooms and the outline of someone."

"Who? The murder victim?"

"No. Someone else. The person is male, I think. He's helping me."

"Helping you do what? Clean up?"

"Quit smoking."

"How does that relate to the murder? Is he the one you think you murdered?"

"No. I think I murdered a young woman."

"Then, how is he relevant?"

"I don't know. I only know the memories of him began coming back at the same time as those of the woman and her murder."

Yvonne rubbed her forehead. "How do you know that you are the one who murdered the girl?"

"I feel rage in the memories. Rage and fear. I know. I just know, I killed her."

"Where do you think this happened?"

"I don't know. I see the inside of a wood cabin. That's it. It's hazy."

"What about the man? Do you know who he is?"

Sheila shook her head. "I don't remember. I didn't even know I'd been a smoker until the memories of the treatment started coming back. It shocked me. I think the treatment must have taken away my memory of being a smoker, as well as having treatment for the habit."

"So, you believe you were a smoker and had treatment?"

"I requested my medical records. They confirm my doctor referred me for help to quit smoking."

"Referred you where?"

"I don't know. The records say nothing, aside from independent hypnotist."

"So, it was hypnotherapy?"

"I believe so, yes."

"Have you asked the surgery whether they know where you they referred you?"

"Yes. My doctor doesn't know. The doctor I was seeing back then died several years ago and no-one else knows where he referred me. He didn't think it necessary to put it in my notes."

"I see. Where were you living, when you had the treatment?"

"Here."

"In Aberystwyth?"

"Yes."

"Okay, well, that's a start." Yvonne leaned back and sighed. "Do you think the murder took place somewhere around here? If it occurred at all?"

"What do you mean, if?" Sheila narrowed her eyes. "I

saw it. I may not have all my memories back, yet, but I know this happened."

"There are such things as false memories. You do know that?"

"I do. This isn't, I'm sure of it. It feels too real."

"Is there anything else you remember about that time in your life?"

"I have bits and pieces. Some of it is vague, while other bits are more lucid. There are bits of discussion with the therapist. New memories come almost every morning and, sometimes, during the day. They often take me by surprise."

"Are you recording the memories as they come?"

"I've been jotting down parts of them in a notebook."

Yvonne nodded. "Good, I'd like you to record everything you remember, as you remember it. I can't do a lot with what you have given me so far, but if I can help you, I will."

"Thank you."

"Have you thought about getting help with recall? Perhaps, another hypnotist?"

"No." Sheila shook her head, her hand coming down onto the table with a thud. "No hypnotist. I'm doing this on my own. I want my memory to come back naturally. It is the only way I can believe in it."

"Do you have someone to support you? This is a big thing to go through on your own."

"I have to do this on my own. I want it that way." Sheila rose from her seat. "Thank you, for listening to me, Inspector."

Yvonne smiled. "No problem. Come back to me, when you know a little more."

∾

TASHA MET the DI in the corridor "What was that all about?"

Yvonne grimaced. "Honestly? I don't know. She's convinced that she murdered another young woman when she, herself, was only twenty years old. She could give me a cursory description of the scene, but not much more than that. She thought it somehow related to treatment she was having to help her stop smoking."

"What?" Tasha raised an eyebrow. "Quit smoking by committing murder? That's an unusual distraction technique if ever I heard one."

"You're hilarious." Yvonne smiled despite herself. "I've asked her to write everything down, as she remembers it, and to come back and see me when she has more. All I have at the moment is a young woman, a cabin, and lots of blood. That's it."

"If it's real, it sounds gruesome."

The DI nodded. "She said, she feels fear and hatred when she remembers. It means she feared and hated the girl she killed, except she doesn't know why. If she remembers enough to give us a location, it would help. In the meantime, if I get any spare time, I may look up unsolved, bloody murders in the Aberystwyth area, circa nineteen-ninety. See what I can find."

3

LOST GIRLS

Rain battered the window as the wind howled and tossed debris around outside.

Yvonne watched the streaks of drizzle develop on the pane and conjoin, her mind wandering over what Sheila Winters had told her.

"Penny for them, ma'am?" Dewi joined her in the CID office in Newtown.

She pursed her lips. "I've been following up a little on Sheila Winter's story." She pushed her glasses atop her head and leaned back in her chair. Now she could focus on the sergeant's face. "I thought I'd look through MisPer files for the Aberystwyth area in the timeframe Sheila outlined."

Dewi sat down. "Did you find anything?"

"Well, several people went missing in the four years either side of 1990. Two of them were young women from the Aberystwyth area. They were, nineteen-year-old Tracy Merrifield, who disappeared after dropping out of college in Aberystwyth, and eighteen-year-old Susan Lee from Borth."

"Really?" Dewi tilted his head, waiting for more.

"Both cases were never officially closed. The two girls never resurfaced."

"Both still missing?"

"Yes."

"You fancy this, then? Cold case work?" Dewi narrowed his eyes. "What if Sheila's info is incorrect? She may have other mental health issues."

The DI tutted. "Thank you, Dewi, I'll bear that in mind. What I need to decide, is how wide to cast the net? Killers like Levi Bellfield and the Shotover Sadist, killed girls from all over the UK. There's no telling whether Sheila's victim was local. It still gets me that several thousand people go missing each year, in the UK, and no-one hears from around three hundred of them ever again. How many of the missing have had their lives violently cut short?"

"Well, don't go too mad, at this stage, in case she isn't the full shilling."

Yvonne rubbed her chin. "I know, she seems convinced of what she is telling me. But, you're right, there's not enough to go on, and the wood cabin could be anywhere or nowhere."

"Was it just two missing girls you found?"

Yvonne shook her head. Altogether, I have found six girls of the right age-group, who went missing within a seven-year time period. No-one has seen them since. The two I told you about, and four others from Powys, including two from Carmarthen. If I widened the net to the whole of Wales, I'd probably find several more. If we do this, I'd like to start with the two from the Aberystwyth area. They are the most likely candidates for Sheila's victim. Hopefully, by the time we get to widening the net, Sheila's memory will have clarified, and she can give us a lot more information. In the meantime, I will speak to Llewelyn and see if we can commit some resources to this."

Dewi pulled a face. "Good luck, with that one."

"COME IN." Llewelyn's voice boomed from the other side of the door. "Aha, Yvonne. Come in. How's it going?"

"Good, I think." She seated herself.

"Did you speak to Brecon drugs squad about the Liverpool gang?"

"I did, sir, and we will liaise with them about the raid. But, that wasn't why I came to see you."

"Oh?" He raised a brow.

"I came to ask if I could spend some time working a cold case. Actually, it may be more than one cold case."

Llewelyn frowned. "Cold case? They are not usually your bag, Yvonne."

"I know, but I have a particular reason to want to investigate this one."

She outlined Sheila Winter's story, apologising that it was all they had, because of Sheila's memory loss.

"Are you saying, she did not know any of this for thirty years? Is that what you are telling me?"

Yvonne nodded. "That's what she says, yes. She tells me she gets a little more of the picture every few days, or so. I hope we'll have a clearer picture before too long."

"Even so..." He grimaced.

"That's not the only reason I want to look into this."

"Go on."

"I began looking for unexplained disappearances of young women in the Aberystwyth area around that time, I found two candidates for Sheila's victim. They were both of similar appearance."

"Really?"

"Both were short in stature, with long blonde hair. They disappeared within eight months of each other."

"I see."

"Four other women, of similar age, disappeared from various locations in Powys. All blonde. All tiny."

Llewelyn rubbed his chin. "And the circumstances of the disappearances?"

"Each was last seen on small roads or lanes, or thought to be at bus stops, or walking between houses or shops, at the time they disappeared. None have turned up again, not in three decades."

"Hmm."

"It's possible these were abductions by a mobile perp, using a vehicle."

"And you think Sheila Winters could have been the abductor?"

"Maybe." Yvonne sighed. "Though, my gut tells me there is more to it. Sheila said, the memories of the murder returned at the same time she remembered the hypnotherapy she had with a male therapist, to help her stop smoking. She is vague with the details. She says she remembers him only in outline and in dimly lit rooms."

"You think he had something to do with the murder?"

"Maybe yes, maybe no, but it is possible."

"Well, it's intriguing, I'll give you that, but as for throwing time and resources at it, I'm not convinced you have enough to go on."

"What about one day per week? I can still get the drugs work done during the other four days."

"A day a week? Just you?"

"If that is all you can spare?"

"For now, I'll agree you can have a day a week on it. If it develops into a concrete case, we can allocate more time and manpower or hand it over to other teams in the area."

"Sure, thank you, sir. I have a feeling it will take a while to access everything Sheila has hidden in her subconscious, if these are true memories."

"Why has it taken so long for her to remember?"

"She doesn't know. She suspects it is something to do with the treatment she had."

"But, if she murdered someone, that is a traumatic experience. Do you think she may have suppressed the bad memories, herself."

Yvonne nodded. "It's something I've considered. Sheila wants to recall the details without help as she is worried about the potential for false memories if she goes to another hypnotist. She is, however, completely convinced of her guilt. She said no-one else was present when she committed the murder."

"Has she got support? It must be one hell of a scary ride she is on."

"I suggested that to her. She tells me she prefers to do this on her own."

"Have you identified her hypnotherapist?"

"Not yet, it's on my list, after finding out the identity of the victim."

"Sheila didn't tell you about other murders she might have been involved in?"

Yvonne shook her head. "She only recalls one murder at the moment. I guess time will tell."

"Okay, well, don't put yourself in any danger. Keep myself and your other colleagues informed of what you are up to. Perhaps, make discreet enquiries with the medical profession regarding Mrs Winters' mental health history. It might give you a better understanding of whether you can trust her story."

"Sure." Yvonne smiled, as she always did when the DCI pointed out the obvious. "I'll keep you updated."

4

ON THE ROAD

"What do you know about hypnosis?" Yvonne asked Tasha, as they relaxed after their evening meal, in front of a log fire.

Tasha tilted her head. "Erm, I know a little, but I am far from an expert on the topic. I know it can be a powerful tool, when used by a skilled therapist."

"Hmm." Yvonne pulled at her lower lip, her eyes half-lidded. "I always doubted the validity of hypnosis I've witnessed in the past."

Tasha laughed. "Well, if all you have seen are the stage shows where the subjects cluck like chicken and eat lemons, I'm not surprised. That is not therapeutic hypnosis. Now, when you hear that hypnosis can be an alternative to anaesthetic for operations, and used to make childbirth a pleasurable experience, you might feel differently."

"Wow, really?" The DI rubbed her chin.

"Really. Like I said, a skilled therapist can enable marked change, the results of which are awe-inspiring."

"Could they make someone commit murder?"

"Gosh, I hope not. But, I guess if the therapist was so

inclined, and they could convince the subject of a need for a murder, it might be possible. You would be better talking to hypnosis experts, though. They would give you a far better picture than I can."

"Oh, I intend to, once I have found some. Out of interest, has someone ever hypnotised you?"

"Me?" Tasha grinned. "No, they have had no reason to. I take it, they haven't hypnotised you either?"

"No. I'm tempted to have a go, though. Find out for myself how powerful it is. I just need to find a good therapist"

"Well, don't go killing anyone, will you?"

The DI laughed. "You are such a spoilsport."

FRIDAY MORNING SAW the DI heading up the coast to Aberystwyth, to speak with Sheila Winters and also chase information regarding the two cold case disappearances from nineteen-ninety.

The sun beat down from a clear sky, quickly melting the thin overnight frost.

"Thank you, for meeting me." Yvonne set down two large mochas, and pulled a couple of bar stools from under the table, in Starbucks cafe on Great Darkgate Street.

They sat facing the plate-glass window, with a view down the street towards North Parade. It was a good place to people-watch, considering all the miscellaneous activities going on along the main road into town.

"I should thank you." Sheila's smile barely curled her thin lips. The lines on her forehead betrayed a troubled inner life.

The DI's voice was soft. "Have you had new memories

since last time we spoke?"

Sheila nodded, her eyes fixed on the window.

"Have you written them down for me?" Yvonne studied the other woman's profile. The crow's feet in the corners of her eyes. The ashen pallor.

"Yes, I am writing them down." Sheila turned to look at her. "The order is all over the place, I'm afraid. I'm not sure about the timeline. What I've got is a collection of memories with no organisation to them. Some appear related to each other, and others standalone. At the moment, I cannot connect them to anything else."

"So, they are dissociated?"

Sheila nodded. "Yes, sometimes the memories are blurred and, over time, become clear. It can take days or even weeks for them to clarify like that. My recall is rather random, I'm afraid."

"I understand. Have you anything to add to what you already told me?"

Sheila scratched her head. "I see a wood with moss, green leaves on the trees, and lots of sunlight coming through the canopy."

"So, it's summer?"

"I believe so, yes."

"Go on."

"I'm carrying something heavy. I think it's an axe. In the memory, I feel happy, like I don't know the horrific thing I am about to do. I hear birds and feel the dappled sunlight on my face. I am dreamlike, as though I don't have a care in the world."

"And, then what?"

"I think I am in this same place, when the rage comes on. Except, it doesn't flow. I mean, I don't see the connection between my happy moments and the ones where I feel angry. All I know is the sun is the same and so is the wood. I can't tell you what makes me rage."

"Do you recognise the wood?"

Sheila shook her head. "No, I don't. Although, in the memory, I know I'm not lost. So, I think I knew the place at the time this murder occurred, like I'd been there before."

"Do you think the axe is the murder weapon?"

"I think it must be, though I haven't recalled the murder itself. I am holding the weapon in the wood and, in a separate memory, there is blood all over the dead woman and the cabin."

"So, how do you know you are the murderer?"

Sheila shrugged. "I feel as though I am responsible in the memory. I'm covered in blood. I know I have killed the girl."

"What about the figure in the dimly lit room? Can you tell me any more about him?"

"I still can't see his face. I don't know what he looks like, but I feel calm in his presence. Calm and warm. Comfortable. I think I like him. Actually, I like him a lot. I feel at home. At peace."

"Can you remember anything he is saying to you?"

"He's asking questions. Things about my past. My early life."

"What sort of things?"

"My relationships with my family and friends, I think. Asking about my dreams and my nightmares."

"Can you remember anything about the room? You said it's dimly lit. What is the light source?"

Sheila closed her eyes, head turning to the side. "Erm, a small lamp, I think, possibly a table lamp. There's also a streetlight outside, whose glow is coming through the window."

"What sort of window?"

"It has lots of small panes. I think it's a sash window."

"So, you could be in a Georgian building?"

Sheila shrugged, opening her eyes. "Maybe."

"You were very young to be needing his help. What age were you when you started smoking?"

Sheila grimaced. "I started when I was twelve. Misspent youth, I'm afraid."

"What made you want to quit?"

"I was engaged, and I wanted to stop before my marriage and, definitely, before becoming pregnant."

"I see. Did you get married?"

She shook her head. "No. The relationship floundered. I broke off the engagement, though I don't remember why. I married someone else, six years later. That's my current husband, Peter."

"Did the ending of your engagement have anything to do with what happened?"

"To the girl? I don't know."

"Okay. So, you're in the dimly lit room. Where is the man in the room?"

Sheila's forehead creased. "Well, initially, I believe he is sitting in the corner. Later, I think he is standing in front of me."

"Are you on a chair?"

"No, I think I am on a bed or a chaise longue."

"Is this all one appointment?"

"I don't know. I think I had many sessions. In some, it is daylight outside. I can't remember anything specific from other sessions. Not yet, anyway."

"Does he touch you?"

"I don't think so. At least, not in what I have remembered so far."

5

WHO WAS THE BLOODIED GIRL?

Seventy-two-year-old Mrs Patricia Merrifield lived alone, in a whitewashed seaside property, along the coast from Aberystwyth harbour.

Yvonne paused before she got to the house to take in the spectacular view of the sea, and of the Llyn Peninsula in the far distance. The air was cold but dry. It tingled her nose till she sneezed, but the sun warmed her face. It seemed a shame to go inside.

She gave the door two solid raps, filling the waiting moments with more of the stunning view.

"Inspector Giles?" Mrs Merrifield opened the door a mere fraction, peering around it.

Yvonne gave her a broad smile. "Yes, Mrs Merrifield." She held out her hand. "Yvonne Giles, CID."

Patricia stepped back, pulling a cream wool blanket tight around her shoulders. "Come in out of the cold."

Yvonne wiped her feet on the doormat.

"Would you like a cup of tea?" Mrs Merrifield asked, as she led the DI through to a bijou, well-equipped kitchen.

"If it's not too much trouble, that would be lovely."

Yvonne's eyes strayed to the window, and more of the sea and the small vessels making the most of it.

"I was brewing one, anyway," Patricia said, taking two mugs from an overhead cupboard.

"Would you like a hand?" Yvonne took a step towards her.

"I'm fine. I'm not decrepit, yet."

"Oh, I didn't mean to imply-"

Mrs Merrifield chuckled. "I know you didn't. You seem far too nice to patronise me."

Yvonne coloured.

"So, why are you looking into my daughter's disappearance again, after all this time?" Patricia asked, as Yvonne carried the tea tray to the kitchen table for her. "I'm not complaining. I'm glad you are. I just thought the police had given up a long time ago."

Yvonne took a sip of her tea. "Someone offered new information. It isn't specifically about your daughter, however. The news concerns an unknown victim. Your daughter is one possibility, and I would like to investigate further. It might enable you to have closure after all these years, though I cannot promise anything."

"She's dead, isn't she?" Patricia's vivid blue eyes searched the DI's face.

"I don't know, Mrs Merrifield, but I think you ought to prepare yourself for that eventuality. I will seek answers, but I cannot guarantee the result will be a happy one."

"Oh, I am prepared. I have been for thirty years. I was never in agreement with the officers investigating previously. They seemed utterly convinced she had run off abroad. All because she had told a friend she would like to explore India."

"I saw that in her file." Yvonne pursed her lips. "But you

don't believe she went away? I read that she dropped out of college two weeks prior to her disappearance. Is that right?"

Patricia nodded. "Tracy was nineteen, with her whole life ahead of her. There were so many avenues open to a girl in her situation, and she seemed genuinely torn between them. She wouldn't have run off without talking to us, though. I was always certain of that. She would tell us her thoughts and had never run away before."

"I understand Tracy was living at home while studying at the university?"

Patricia nodded. "She was. We earned enough income that she didn't qualify for a student grant, but were actually too poor to afford her accommodation fees. Living with us and studying in Aberystwyth was the obvious solution."

"Did she enjoy her subject?"

"International Politics? Yes, she did. She had always shown an interest in what was going on in the world. When she was twelve, we bought a black and white television set for her room. Only a small thing, it was, but she used to watch the news and any wildlife series on it. She liked public and political debates. I would hear her arguing with the telly often."

"So, what made her give up her studies, Mrs Merrifield?"

"Pat, please."

"Sorry, Pat."

"I don't know. It took me by surprise. I tried talking her round, but she seemed determined that it was no longer what she wanted."

"What was she going to do next, did she say?"

Pat shook her head. "She didn't, but she told me that it would take her a few months to make her mind up. That was ten days before her disappearance."

"What happened the day she vanished? Can you walk me through it from the start?"

"Sure. We got up around seven in the morning. My husband and I."

Yvonne looked at the notes she had brought with her. "Your husband, that would be Terry?"

"Yes, he died, aged forty-eight. He never stopped looking for her. Almost seven years, he spent almost every waking minute searching, until his death of heart failure." Pat's eyes were half-lidded. A lone tear made its way down her cheek as her chin trembled.

"I'm so sorry." Yvonne reached out to place a hand on top of Pat's. "The pair of you must have been beside yourselves."

"For months, I barely slept. When I did, I dreamed about her coming through the door, telling me about her day. Waking up was the cruellest thing."

"I bet. I can't even imagine the pain you went through every day."

Pat drew in a large breath as though to refocus. "So, we got up about seven. Tracy got up around eight. I called her down for her breakfast. She liked egg on toast."

"I see."

"She ate her breakfast and then worried that her dad only had a tiny amount of milk left for his cereal. She offered to get some. Said she would get a magazine while she was at it. National Geographic, I think. That was one she frequently bought."

"You weren't living here at the time? The address is different."

Pat stroked the back of her hair, gazing out of the window. "We lived in a townhouse on Penglais Road. We stayed there until Terry Passed away. We didn't want to leave that house in case she came home. That was the home she knew. But, when Terry died, I struggled there on my own. So many empty rooms. It was too big and too empty for me. This cottage suited me better. For years, I would pop by the old home to ask whether my daughter had been there."

"So, you made the move. I can't say I blame you. I would have done the same. Coming back to the day she disappeared, what time did she leave the house?"

"It would have been somewhere between eight-twenty and eight-thirty. She had been to the Spar shop at the bottom of North Parade many times. She could be there and back in fifteen minutes. After an hour passed, we worried, but thought she might have bumped into someone on the way. By two o'clock, however, I was worrying so much, I phoned the police. Terry went to the shop to ask if she had been in. She hadn't. That was when I panicked. It wasn't like her. Even if she had wanted to go off, she would have made sure that her dad had his milk first. That's the sort of girl she was. Tracy didn't like to let anyone down."

"From the original police enquiries, I can see that no-one witnessed her being taken, but someone saw her leaving your garden and setting off down the road."

"Yes, they were in a car and saw her at the gate, but only for a few moments."

"If I can trace that couple, I would like to speak to them about the sighting, myself."

"Are the details in her file?"

"Their address at the time is in there, yes. I'll start from there."

"Do you think someone abducted her, Inspector?"

Yvonne pursed her lips. "From what you are telling me, I would think it very possible."

"Because she disappeared ten days after dropping out of

college, the police at the time felt she might have wanted to disappear. They said a girl fitting her description had boarded a train at Aberystwyth station. But, when I saw the description of the clothing, I knew it wasn't Tracy. She was wearing a blue raincoat, not a purple one, and she hadn't been carrying a bag. She took her purse in her coat pocket."

"And they never found the purse?"

"No."

"Why did she leave college?"

"She decided the course wasn't for her. She also wanted money and thought getting a job would benefit her more. She wanted to campaign with local election candidates, and thought that she night run for council, herself."

"What sort of employment was she considering?"

"She wrote, in her spare time, and fancied working for a local newspaper. She'd been around most of the local offices asking whether they would consider taking her on. Some of them had given favourable responses, telling her they would keep her details on file. She knew she was unlikely to get a position straight away, so she was happy for that. In the meantime, she was considering employment in bars and restaurants and the local supermarkets. She had a lot of energy and could make things happen. Tracy was ever the optimist."

"She sounds like a wonderful daughter."

"She was. She is. Wherever she is."

"I know." Yvonne pulled at her lower lip.

"Will you find out what happened to her?" Pat's round eyes emphasised her plea.

"I can tell you that I will try my best." The DI smiled, tilting her head. "But, you know I can't promise to get an answer, don't you?"

Pat nodded. "I know, but if you promise to try, that is

good enough. I can see that you mean what you say, Inspector. You have a lovely manner."

"Thank you." Yvonne gave her card to Pat. "I want you to call me. Any time, night or day, if you think of anything you would like me to know. I would be glad of the help and I will always answer when able. If I cannot answer straight away, I'll get back to you as soon as I can."

"Thank you, Inspector." Pat placed the card on her kitchen table. "I will."

Yvonne rose to leave. "Thank you for your time, Mrs Merrifield. I'm sure I will speak to you again before too long. If I discover new information, relevant to your daughter, you will be the first to know."

As she left, the DI desperately wanted closure for Pat Merrifield. Despite this, she hoped that Pat's daughter was not the girl hacked to death by sheila Winters. It had to be someone's daughter; she knew that. Whoever the parents of Sheila's victim were, her manner of death would devastate them. Yvonne knew that she would likely be the one informing them of it. It was hardest thing, to be the bearer of such dreadful news.

Less than five miles from Pat Merrifield, Mr and Mrs Lee lived in Borth, another seaside town just along the coast from Aberystwyth. Their eighteen-year-old Daughter, Susan, had disappeared within six months of Tracy Merrifield. Now retired, they still lived in the house on the seafront where Susan grew up.

Yvonne parked her car in a marked bay abutting the seawall and walked the thousand yards to their home.

She cleared her throat before ringing the bell.

Tom Lee, Susan's father, opened the door.

As Yvonne greeted him, showing her ID, he stared for a moment, saying nothing. His eyes betrayed a reluctance to hear news. Perhaps, the DI mused, because he had had his hopes raised before, only to have them dashed like the rocks being relentlessly worn down by the sea. She understood.

"Is that the inspector?" A female voice came from behind him.

"Yes," he answered, before running a hand through his thinning grey hair, and turning back to Yvonne. "Please, come in."

"Thank you." She unbuttoned her coat but didn't take it off.

He led her through to a large and airy lounge with two immense bay windows. The light and warmth lifted her despite the gravity of her visit.

"Have you had news?" Cathy Lee came towards her, grey hair neatly coiffed, her face made-up, her gait unsteady.

Yvonne tilted her head. "I don't have information specific to your daughter, Mrs Lee, I'm afraid. But, we have new information that I am following up. It might relate to disappearances from the area. I can't really tell you any more than that at this stage."

"I see." Cathy's face fell. "We've gotten our hopes up so many times over the years."

"I know. It must have been hard for you. I came to ask you about Susan. I see from the case file that she had a history of running away."

Tom Lee tutted, flicking his head. "They used that as an excuse not to investigate."

Yvonne cleared her throat. "I thought they carried out initial enquiries around the town?"

"Their heart wasn't in it. They thought she had run off again. They kept telling us she would come back."

The DI nodded. "I'm sorry. I understand why they might have believed that, but it must have been frustrating for you."

Cathy held onto her husband's arm as she lowered herself onto the sofa.

Tom Lee motioned Yvonne to an armchair as he took a seat next to his wife.

"We still wait for Susan to come through that door." Cathy gazed through the window towards the front of the house.

"Is that your daughter?" The DI pointed to a photograph on the mantle of a young girl around six years of age, with a gap in her front teeth.

"Yes." Cathy smiled, her expression a mixture of pride and sadness.

"How often did she run away?"

"Oh, she went every few months. She would get frustrated with us or with school or, sometimes, she would simply want an adventure. Susan was a tomboy, through and through. Our girl was always climbing trees and going on adventures. But she never went far. She would camp out in a friends garden for a night or two, and then she would be back."

"I see that she was eighteen when she disappeared the final time?" Yvonne read from her notes.

"Yes, she had been working in the fish and chip shop down the road. She liked the people she worked with, but the job wasn't for her. Susan wanted to do something exciting, she just didn't know what. She was thinking about college when she disappeared. She fancied marine biology, but she wasn't academic in school. Examinations were stressful for her."

"Talk to me about the day she disappeared. Tell me as much as you can remember."

"We'd had breakfast and Susan wanted to catch the bus to Aberystwyth. She had friends in the town and intended meeting them for some shopping and then a few drinks."

"Did she have a boyfriend?"

"She had boys who were chasing her, but she didn't have anyone serious that we knew of. I think the police went through her male friends in their initial investigation."

"Sure. What time did she set off?"

"Around nine that morning. She was aiming to get the bus that left at nine-twenty. I had prepared sandwiches for her to take in her bag because she had barely touched her breakfast. She wasn't good at eating first thing in the morning. Susan was only seven stone."

"I see. Did you hear from her again that day?"

Cathy shook her head. "No, mobile phones were not a thing back then. She could have used a payphone, but she wouldn't have felt the need to call. Susan was intending being back home by ten o'clock."

"I understand that her friends didn't see her. She didn't meet them where and when she said she would."

"That's right, they waited for her at the bus station. Each time a bus from Borth was due, they thought she would be on it. They eventually gave up, thinking she must have changed her mind."

"But you were sure she wouldn't have done that?"

"I know she wouldn't have. Susan hadn't run away for years. She had grown into a sensible girl who cared about her friends and didn't like hurting other people's feelings. She would not have left them waiting around by choice."

"What do you think happened?"

"We think someone took her from the bus stop. The bus driver was adamant she wasn't there when he did his pickup. We believe they either offered her a lift or forced her into a vehicle before the bus was due."

"Had she ever complained about being stalked?"

Tom shook his head. "No, never."

"Did she have any local friends who could drive?"

"She had one-or-two, but we phoned around and spoke to those and they said they hadn't seen her. They were young lads who still lived with their parents. It was a Saturday. They hadn't left the house."

"I see. Did anyone see Susan waiting at the bus stop?"

Cathy nodded. "There was an elderly couple who said that they saw her eating a sandwich and looking at her watch. That was around ten minutes before the bus was due. They didn't stop to talk to her. They said she looked relaxed and happy."

"When did you realise something was wrong?"

"We didn't until ten-thirty that night. The last bus had been and gone, and there was no sign of Susan. I had a terrible sinking feeling. I just knew something wasn't right." Cathy looked to her husband for affirmation. "I told you, didn't I?"

He nodded. "We didn't know what to do. I telephoned the police who said they couldn't do anything until the next day, as she may have stayed over in Aberystwyth after a few drinks with her friends-"

Cathy interjected. "I knew something was wrong. She would have telephoned to let us know that she was staying over and not coming home. She knew I fretted and, like I said, she was much more sensible as she grew up. Susan didn't like worrying people."

"What is the new information you have?" Tom Lee asked, his eyes narrowed.

Yvonne pursed her lips, smoothing her skirt with her hands. "Someone has come forward, saying that she lost her memory thirty years ago. Memories have come back to her, and they involve something happening to a young woman. She can't say who, yet, and your daughter is not the only candidate. I wouldn't get your hopes up, but I intend to investigate the disappearances of the young women, in the light of the statements from this witness. She is giving me the new information as she remembers it. I will do my best to find the answers and, perhaps, give families some closure."

As the DI was about to leave, Cathy called out. "There was something else. Another young girl reported a man pulling her by the arm, at the bus stop our daughter disappeared from."

Yvonne stopped in her tracks. "Go on..."

"She was waiting for the bus, and a car pulled up close to the curb. The driver motioned her over. She thought he meant to ask her for directions, but he didn't. Instead, he pulled hard on her arm, so that her head almost hit the car."

"She asked him what he thought he was doing, and he apologised and said he had thought she was someone else."

"Was he trying to get her inside the vehicle?"

Cathy shook her head. "She didn't think so. The car door was closed. He'd reached through his driver's window, which he'd wound all the way down."

"Who was the girl?"

"Delia Evans."

"Does she still live around here?"

"I think she runs the novelty shop down the road, Tom, doesn't she?"

Tom nodded. "She's Delia Randle, now. That's her married name. She's owned the bucket and spade shop for the last ten years."

"Thank you. I'd like to talk to her. What did she tell you about the vehicle?"

"She didn't tell us. We read it in the local newspaper. She thought it was a mustard car, possibly a Mini. Police talked to owners of mustard-coloured Minis and said they had no reason to suspect any of wrong-doing. So, that was that. We thought the incident related, however. I couldn't help wondering if that was what happened to Susan. Maybe someone pulled her into that car."

"It seems curious, I'll admit." Yvonne nodded. "When did Delia's incident happen? How long after your daughter's disappearance?"

"About three months, not much more than that. It was late summer or early autumn."

"I see."

As she left, Yvonne decided she would speak to Delia Randle right away.

Yvonne waited for the two people ahead of her to finish being served.

Delia Randle looked tired but relaxed. Yvonne estimated her to be around fifty years old from the flecks of grey in her shoulder-length auburn hair, and the crow's feet developing at her temples. Her wedding and engagement rings had sunken into the flesh of her fingers, almost like the wire of a fence, dug into a tree, as the tree carries on growing around it.

"Can I help you?"

Yvonne jumped, looking up into curious brown eyes.

"You were miles away."

The DI grinned. "Sorry, I was off in my own little world. Are you Delia?"

The other woman tilted her head. "Yes, I am. Why?"

"Aha, I am DI Yvonne Giles. I'm investigating disappearances of young women, from this region, thirty years ago."

"Okay." Delia bit her lip. "Why have you come to me?"

Yvonne cleared her throat. "Is it okay to talk here?"

Delia looked around. No other shoppers had come through the door. "Yes, here is fine."

"I understand you were involved in a strange incident at the bus stop in Borth in the period I am interested in."

Delia's forehead creased. "You mean the guy who pulled me towards his car?"

"Yes. Do you remember what he looked like?"

"He was a white man and dark-haired, I think. He wore smart-casual clothing. A shirt and thin jumper, if I remember correctly."

"What colour was the jumper?"

"Green? I think. A darkish green."

"Age?"

"I don't know... Thirties? Mid-thirties, I would say."

"Did he have facial hair?"

Delia shook her head. "Not that I recall. I didn't see him for more than a moment. When he pulled me, I felt shocked and scared. "

"Did he try to pull you through the window?"

"No, it was more a kind of yanking of my arm, almost like he wanted to take it out of its socket."

"What did he say to you?"

"Nothing at first. But, when I asked him what he was playing at, he let me go, and apologised, saying he had mistaken me for somebody else."

"I see. Do you remember anything else about the vehicle, inside or out?"

"It was a light-coloured Mini."

"You said, when police interviewed you, that you thought it was tan."

"Yes, a sort of mustard colour."

"But, it was definitely a Mini that you saw?"

"I believe so. I was so shocked at him pulling me, I didn't pay that much attention to the car."

"But you reported it?"

"Well, not straight away. I remembered the incident when police were making enquiries after Susan Lee went missing. They wanted to know why I waited until then to say something. I got the impression they felt I might be attention-seeking. I wasn't. It really happened."

Yvonne nodded. "Of course. Did you see him drive away?"

"Erm, yes. I did."

"Which direction did he go?"

"He turned round and headed back away from the seafront, like he was maybe intending to drive out of Borth."

"Had you seen him or his vehicle before?"

"No, I hadn't."

"What about after?"

"No, I never saw him after that."

Yvonne handed Delia her card. "I may need to speak with you again, at some point. In the meantime, if you remember anything else, would you call me on that number?"

"Yes, sure." Delia pocketed the card, just as her next customer came through the door.

LATER THAT EVENING, Yvonne related the Delia Randle incident to Tasha.

"So, he wasn't trying to pull her into his vehicle?"

"She says not. His window was open, but the car door was closed. He tugged hard on her arm, then apologised when she questioned him. Said he'd mistaken her for someone else."

"Hmm." Tasha rubbed her chin, eyes half-lidded.

"What are you thinking?" The DI asked, her gaze searching Tasha's face.

"Well, like I say, I am no expert, but what you were saying about hypnosis..."

"Yes?"

"There's a style of hypnosis that's said to influence people in normal conversation. You can put a person into a trance-like state without them realising what is happening."

"Really?"

"Yes. It's known as the Ericksonian method, after the guy who started it. If my memory is correct."

"Okay..."

"Basically, if you shock a person, you can put them in a trance. It may not work on everyone, nor every time, but anything that kick starts your brain into trying to work out what is happening, has the potential to put you into a hypnotic state."

"I see. So, you think the yanking of Delia's arm may have been an attempt to send her into a trance?"

"Yes, people go into trance all the time. They just don't

realise it. The last time you drove several miles and couldn't remember having done so, you were in a trance. Daydreaming is a trance-like state. Stunning someone can send them into trance long enough for a practised hypnotist to speak directly to their subconscious."

"Wow, I see. That sounds like a powerful technique."

"It can be. Like I said, I am no expert on hypnosis and I am only telling you this because you said Sheila Winters had been seeing a hypnotherapist. I suggest you get talking to therapeutic experts unlinked to the case as soon as you can. Find out what hypnosis is capable of. Do you know who Sheila's hypnotherapist was?"

The DI shook her head. "Not yet, but I will soon. I am working alone on this, at the moment, one day a week. So it's taking more time than usual to work my way through all the information. I'm hoping the DCI will resource the investigation better as I make progress."

Tasha nodded. "Let me know if I can help you. I can do whatever you need."

Yvonne smiled, giving her partner a hug. "Thank you. I appreciate it."

6

SECRET HELPER

In Newtown, the following day, Yvonne caught up with Dewi. "How's it going?" she asked, as they took five minutes with a cuppa.

"Missed you, yesterday." Dewi plopped his mug on the table. It was strange, taking my orders from a DI in Brecon."

"Have the drugs squad settled on a date for the raid?"

Dewi nodded. "They're going for small hours, on the fifteenth."

Yvonne nodded. "It'll put a major dent in the gang operations round here. Hopefully, they won't recover from it for a few years."

Dewi grimaced. "We can hope. Problem is, as you know, we'll get rid of the Liverpool lot and another gang will come from somewhere else."

"And we're on the edge of the merry-go-round with our feet pressed to the floor."

"Exactly." Dewi searched her face. "What about this mysterious murder case you've landed in Aberystwyth, eh? What's going on with that? You've been unusually silent about it."

"Lots, and not very much, Dewi." Yvonne pursed her lips. "I have to say, It's a fascinating case and I am dying to get to the bottom of it. However, my self-confessed murderess has a memory full of holes. Her recall is tantalisingly vague. God only knows if we will get anything useful from it. I met the mother of one of the missing women, the other day, though, and I really felt for her."

"She's been waiting for answers a long time."

"Exactly. Sheila Winters might be the key to getting them. I have this suspicion she was being coerced by someone with undue influence. A killer-by-proxy, if you will, responsible for whatever Sheila did. She thinks she was being hypnotised at the time these events occurred, and that is one helluva coincidence. I could be wrong. The hypnotherapist might be innocent, and Sheila could have killed another woman out of jealousy or something. If only she could remember what the young woman looked like, so we could get an artist's impression. Something we could take to the families of the missing."

"Or we could find the bodies, if they're dead."

"Yes, key to that, would be Sheila remembering where her supposed murder mission took place. She sees it in a wood, but doesn't know which wood."

"Does she know who her hypnotist was?"

Yvonne shook her head. "She doesn't, Dewi. So, my next step will be to root through old papers, clinic logs, and so on, to find out who was operating in that area in nineteen-ninety. Might take a while to find them all. Then I've got to hope that Sheila can recognise one of them."

"Do you need help?" Her DS tilted his head, his forehead lined in concentration.

"That's a kind offer, Dewi, but I don't think the DCI would approve."

"Well, I won't tell him if you don't. I can give you an hour or two here and there, can't I? And, if it's research, I won't have to stick to Fridays, like you're having to."

Yvonne grinned. "*If* I stick to them. To be honest, I doubt I'll be able to interview all the people on my on a single day a week. Not all of them will be available on the same day."

"Let's hope the DCI see sense, before you get that far." Dewi took a gulp from his tea.

"Yes, but it depends on me getting a lot more to go on than I have at the moment, and that's what worries me. It's a catch twenty-two."

7

HYPNOTHERAPY

"I've got a name for you, ma'am. An independent hypnotherapist who is still working in the Aberystwyth area and has been since the mid-eighties."

"Well done, Dewi, that is excellent news." Yvonne beamed at him.

"I'd lay bets on her knowing others that worked around the area, too, and anyone still working." Dewi pushed his chest out, hands in his trouser pockets while rocking back and forth on his heels.

"And very smug you look too, Hughes." Yvonne grinned, patting him on the back. "Good job. Who is it? And how do I contact them?"

Dewi led her over to his desk. "Her name is Susan Owen. She's sixty-eight and still working. Tells me she has no intentions of retiring and plans to continue working for a few years yet."

"So, she would have been thirty-eight at the time Sheila was being seen by a male colleague?"

"Right."

"How do I contact her?"

"I have her phone number here, ma'am." Dewi copied the name and number from his notebook onto a post-it. "There you go. Don't tell me that I do nothing for you."

"You are a superstar, Dewi Hughes. I owe you a beer or two."

Her sergeant placed his hands on his hips. "You said that last time. I'm still waiting."

Yvonne pointed to his notebook. "Add them to the tab," she advised, grinning as she ducked out of the office to make the call on her mobile.

SUSAN OWEN GREETED the DI with a smile that lit her face as she opened the porticoed front door to her home, off Penglais Hill, in Aberystwyth.

Her hand was steady as she extended it. A tightly curled bun held up her greying hair and, with her prominent cheekbones, long fingers and slender outline, she had a refined, cultured appearance as though she had stepped out of a painting or come down from a sculptor's platform.

Yvonne Accepted the handshake, with a smile. The DI hoped she would look as good as Susan did at sixty-eight, as she introduced herself. "This is a beautiful place, Mrs Owens. Yvonne cast her eyes over the oil paintings, in gilt frames, in the generously sized cream hallway, finally letting them rest on the yellow-and-black tiled, Victorian floor."

"Thank you, Inspector. And it's Susan, please."

The DI smiled. "And I am Yvonne."

"Yvonne, that's a nice name. Would you like a cup of tea?"

"Do you know what? I would love one, thank you." She followed the elegant woman along the hall to the kitchen.

This room was also an impressive size and well kitted out. Everything appeared perfectly made to measure.

"Do you live alone?" Yvonne asked, musing that it was a large place for any one person to look after, let alone someone older in years.

"I do now, since my husband passed away."

"Oh, gosh, I'm sorry, I-"

Susan held her hand up. "It's all right, it's been a while. I have a cleaner who comes in once a week," she added, as though reading the DI's thoughts.

Yvonne felt the colour rise in her cheeks.

"My clients keep me fully occupied. I don't have time to dwell. I unwind by attending yoga."

"How long have you been a hypnotherapist?" Yvonne asked, watching Susan pour hot water into a bright orange Clarice Cliff teapot.

"Oh, forty years, something like that. I got into it when hypnotism was becoming popular for a variety of conditions, back in the days when the public still thought it akin to black magic."

"I must admit it has always been a mystery to me." Yvonne grimaced.

"You are not alone." Susan passed her a cup and saucer.

The DI smiled. It was a pleasure to sip tea from traditional crockery. She hadn't done so in a long time.

"So, how can I help you, Inspector?"

Yvonne took a sip of the hot tea. "I'm investigating the disappearances of young women that happened thirty years ago. I have a witness who tells me that she is having memories which could help me, but she lost part of her memory while having hypnotherapy treatment in nine-teen-ninety. She tells me the treatment was supposed to erase her memory of the condition, for which she was being treated, but she believes she forgot more than intended."

Susan frowned. "I see."

"I was wondering if you could tell me who was working in this area as a hypnotherapist back then. Specifically, I am interested in male colleagues. I would also like to pick your brains about hypnotism and hypnotherapy, if I may?"

"Do you think the disappearance of the girls involved a male hypnotherapist? Were they being hypnotised?" Susan asked, focussing on Yvonne's face. "Or are you simply interested in the reasons for your subject's memory loss?"

"I am not saying I believe it involved the therapist, but I would like to speak to the one who was treating my witness about her memory loss, yes. She is recalling her therapist for the first time, and this is coinciding with her recall of what happened to a young woman, who may be one of several missing girls. The memories seem linked in a way she cannot yet explain. I would like to help her get to the bottom of her memories and perhaps solve a cold case."

"I see. Would she like help to access the memories? Would that be something helpful? I would happily do that kind of work."

Yvonne shook her head. "At the moment, she would not. She is afraid of having false memories and thinks there is less chance of that if she has natural recall."

Susan frowned. "Personally, I don't believe that false memories are as large a factor as we have made them out to be. But, I understand her reluctance. I could make myself available, however, if she changes her mind."

"Thank you." Yvonne rubbed her chin. "That is very kind and would be very helpful."

Susan finished her tea, placing her mug and saucer down onto the Indian rosewood coffee table in front of them. "As for the colleagues working here thirty years ago, I can recall four altogether. Many of them are still working."

"Okay."

"Let's see now, there's George Langley. He was married to a lovely woman from Clarach. He would have been around forty in nineteen-ninety. He had his own clinic on the industrial estate. I believe he rented out space to another colleague, Brian Watson, who would have been mid-thirties. The two of them became business partners and have run a joint clinic ever since. As I recall, Brian had just gotten divorced in the late eighties."

"One moment..." Yvonne was scribbling hard to make sure she had it all down.

"Then there was Simon Hopkins. He worked and works mainly from home, though he visited NHS clinics from time-to-time. The others did, too, but less often. He was married, I believe. And the last one was Hefin Thomas, who worked from home, much like myself. He would have been mid-forties. I'm afraid Hefin died several years ago. His wife lives in the same house where he did most of his work."

"I'm impressed at your memory." Yvonne smiled.

Susan raised an eyebrow. "I may be older, Yvonne, but I still have all my faculties."

The DI coloured. "Oh, I didn't mean to imply-"

Susan laughed. "It's okay, I was teasing you."

"Oh." Yvonne shifted in her seat.

"I may have photos of them in an old album. We went to a lot of conferences and training together. We also met up at Christmas, most years. I am sure I could lay my hands on images of all of them. Would you like me to look?"

"Could you?" Yvonne's eyes lit up. "That would be incredibly helpful, if it's not too much trouble."

"Of course I could." Susan smiled, rising from the sofa.

"You stay there and finish your tea, and I will get the albums from the library."

Yvonne was not at all surprised by Susan Owen having a library room in her house. It fit with the house and the woman. "Is hypnotherapy a lucrative career?" She asked, immediately regretting her cheekiness.

Susan tilted her head as she looked back. "My husband was a professor at the university and patented a purification procedure that netted him a lot of money. What you see is, in large part, owed to that rather than my meagre income. However, there are some parts of my job that pay better."

Yvonne grimaced. "I'm sorry, I had no right to pry."

Susan smiled, turning away towards the library. "It's fine, it's your job to pry," she answered.

WHEN THE HYPNOTHERAPIST RETURNED, she held three albums.

The DI helped her place them onto the coffee table. "Are all of them still working?" She enquired.

Susan nodded. "I believe so Simon Hopkins still works from home, though he travels around the country sometimes. He has a website and gets a lot of interest that way. I think he does therapy via the internet, too."

"Any others?"

"Brian Watson works, though I think it is only part-time, now. I believe he still does NHS work."

"And what about George Langley?"

"I haven't heard from George for a while. I think he is still working. As far as I know, he still has the clinic on the industrial estate with Brian."

Susan flicked through the albums, pausing now and then to remove photos from under the thin films of plastic.

She spread the images on the table. "There they are," she said. "Would I be able to have these photographs back when you have finished with them?"

"Yes, of course." Yvonne nodded. "I'll have them digitised, and will get them returned to you as soon as I can."

"Oh, good." Susan smiled. "There are a lot of memories in these albums."

"I'm sure." Yvonne nodded. "Would you be so kind as to write the names on the back of them?"

Susan held up a pencil. "I thought you might ask me that. I came prepared."

The DI grinned. "Great minds think alike."

Sheila scribbled the names and events on the backs of the photographs, before handing them to Yvonne. "Will that be all, Inspector? Only, I am expecting a client in ten minutes and I need to get the room ready."

"There was one more thing." Yvonne ran a hand through her hair. "Can you recall if any of these men drove a mustard-coloured vehicle back then? Possibly, a Mini?"

Susan frowned. "A mustard-coloured vehicle... It doesn't ring any bells, Yvonne. I'll have to think about it and get back to you."

"Of course." Yvonne rose to go, her knees clicking as she did. "I wanted to speak to you again sometime, anyway. I'd like to pick your brains about hypnotism if I could."

"Yes, that's absolutely fine." Susan nodded. "Just call me and let me know whether we can do it by phone, or you need to see me in person, and I'll make sure I put you in the diary. Either would be okay with me, clients permitting."

Yvonne smiled. "Thank you so much, Susan. It's been a pleasure."

Susan saw the DI out. "Likewise, Inspector."

LATER THAT DAY, Yvonne sat in CID, examining the photographs. Some were old back-and-whites, but most were colour. The quality was easily good enough for her to show them to Sheila Winters, which she intended doing in the hopes it would jog Sheila's memory about the hypnotherapy sessions and their relationship to her other memories.

In them, George Langley wore a tweed jacket, shirt and tie in his photograph. A pipe hung loosely from his jaw as he chatted away to others, hands in his trouser pockets.

Brian Watson appeared more casual in his photo, sporting a neckerchief, waistcoat, and shoulder-length brown hair. He appeared lean and taller than the others.

Simon Hopkins wore a shirt and tie, his sleeves rolled up to the elbows. His hair, short at the sides and longer at the back. The DI smiled to herself. Definitely a mullet.

Hefin Thomas wore a flat-cap and tweed jacket. He looked very much the country gent in his photograph. Yvonne wondered what he had done when he wasn't working. She suspected he had come from a farming family. Perhaps lived on a farm. He appeared full of life, his face animated in mid-conversation, as he had been in the photo. The DI felt saddened to think he was now deceased.

Photographs had that power. The power to transport you, like a time-traveller, to an earlier world. To see things as they were and not as they are. Giving, at once, both insight and a voyeuristic knowledge of another's history. The light that burnished these images had bounced off those individuals, in that place and time, captured forever.

"Penny for them?" Dewi interrupted her flow.

"Oh, Dewi." She put a hand to her chest. "I didn't hear you approach..."

"That's because you were miles away, ma'am. Are you all right? You were looking sad."

"I was in a bit of a trance for a moment, Dewi. I think I had hypnotised myself." She grinned.

"Had you?" He frowned.

"I had. I am reliably informed that when you're carried away with your own thoughts like that, it is a lot like hypnosis."

"Well, in that case, I think you are in a hypnotic trance often." Dewi grinned. "The next time I see you in that state, I'll whisper in your ear that you would like to make the next round of tea and coffee for everyone in the office."

Yvonne pulled a face. "You are hilarious, aren't you?" She pursed her lips. "Don't you dare try it, though? What if it worked? I'd never live it down."

Dewi laughed. "It would be funny. You'd better keep your wits about you, just in case."

"While you're there, Dewi. You couldn't do me a favour when you have a bit of time, could you?"

"Is it a hush-hush favour?" Dewi winked at her.

"Yes, better not let the DCI get wind of it at this stage."

"What do you want me to do?" he asked, seating himself on the edge of her desk.

"Well, I have four more names for hypnotherapists who were working in the Aberystwyth area in nineteen-ninety. Susan Owens jotted down where they had their offices. Can you chase them up for me? Get a few details around where they are now, and set up meetings for me, if you can. I know one of them, Hefin Thomas, is deceased. The others are still around. As usual, any meetings will need to be on a Friday, for now. Can you do that?"

"I'll get on it as soon as I can. Any idea when you'll have enough to persuade Llewelyn to let the team loose on this?"

Yvonne shook her head. "No, but I don't expect it'll be in the next week or two. Not unless Sheila Winters has a few more significant memories surface, and I just don't know if that will happen."

"She hasn't identified the wood yet, then?" Dewi jumped down off the desk.

"Not yet. I'll be speaking to her by phone, later, but I can't see her in person until next Friday. It's difficult making progress when the time is so limited."

Dewi needed. "I know, but you're doing a good job so far. Something will come up soon, I'm sure. It usually does."

Yvonne nodded. "Thanks, Dewi."

8

SOMETHING AND NOTHING

The following Friday morning, Yvonne met Sheila in reception at Aberystwyth police station. "Thank you for coming," she said, ushering her through to an interview room.

"I haven't got long," Sheila apologised. "I'm meeting a friend for a spot of shopping and lunch. I haven't seen her for almost six months and today was the only day she could do."

Yvonne flicked a look at her watch. It was half-past nine. "What time are you meeting her?"

Sheila grimaced. "Ten."

"I see. Well, we had better get on with it then." The DI spread the photographs out on the table. "Sheila, take a really good look at these images. I want you to tell me if you recognise someone in any of them. Take all the time you need."

Sheila nodded, placing her handbag down on the floor beside her and slipping her coat off onto the back of her chair.

Yvonne watched as Mrs Winters cast her eyes over them one-by-one, pausing over each to study them, her face lined in concentration. It was clear she had had her nails and hair done for the shopping trip. The muted red polish on the manicured nails matched her lipstick. Her hair had been cut and waved.

Sheila sat back in her chair, looking at the DI.

"Anything?" Yvonne asked, leaning in.

She shook her head, her mouth curling down at the corners. "I'm sorry, I just don't recognise anyone."

"No-one at all?"

Sheila shook her head.

"Flip each photo over, and look at the names on the back. See if that helps jog your memory."

Sheila took her time. It was clear to Yvonne that the woman wanted to help, but nothing was jumping out at her. She spent minutes going over them all again. "I'm sorry," she said, finally. "I'm just not getting anything. No memory. No response. I don't recognise any of them."

"I see." Yvonne pursed her lips. "Don't worry, Sheila. It will probably take time and require more of your memory to return-"

"Perhaps, If you showed photographs of them working? Or photographs of them in dimly lit rooms? In my memory, I am seeing an outline. I'm really not remembering much more than that."

Yvonne nodded. "And yet, you would have met, presumably, in a well-lit space when you were looking into having therapy with them, wouldn't you?"

Sheila nodded. "Yes, I must have met them in the light. I just can't remember."

"It's curious." Yvonne scratched her head. "I wonder why you can't remember your therapist? Is it related to the traumatic experience you think took place later on, or did someone make it so you couldn't remember?"

Sheila shrugged. "I don't know."

"And the names don't help?"

"I haven't got a name in my head. Not one."

"Are you dreaming at all?"

"Yes."

"Are you writing them down?"

"Not the dreams, I'm not, no. I didn't think I needed to note them down. However, I am writing up the memories, just as you asked me to."

"Okay. Have you had anything more come through about the wood where you think the murder took place?"

Sheila shook her head. "I've had more memories of walking there. I can see my surroundings reasonably well, but it could be any wood. I have seen the hut from outside, but it could be any old shack. I mean, there is nothing to distinguish it. It's a little broken down, the guttering is falling off at one end. That's it. If only I could see myself approaching the wood. I might see a sign or recognise the landscape, but that hasn't happened, yet."

"That's okay. Look, these things take time. Try to relax and don't force it. It will come. In the meantime, I am talking to therapists, to see if I can locate yours. One of us will find something that moves things forward, I'm sure."

Sheila nodded.

Yvonne checked her watch. "Time has gone on, you'd better get off to meet your friend, it's almost ten o'clock."

As Mrs Winters scurried out of the station, returning briefly for her forgotten coat. Yvonne wondered whether she was wasting her time. Even if she were to find the therapist, if Sheila's memory didn't yield something more than it had, it was hard to see how anything could move forward. And, without evidence of murder, all she had was the missing girls with nothing to warrant a full reopening of their thirty-year-old cases.

"YOU'RE DYING to make coffee for everyone in the office and you want to do it, now." Dewi whispered in her ear.

"Dewi Hughes, give over." Yvonne laughed, giving him a push. "I may have looked like I was zoned-out, but I actually wasn't, so there."

"Damn." Dewi put on a mock-hurt expression. "I really thought I'd got you then."

The DI grinned. "You should have waited another couple of minutes. I'd have been in full flow."

"Oh, trust me to get my timing all wrong." Dewi tutted, tossing his head. "There's always a next time. Anyway, you'll be pleased to hear, I got hold of three of your therapist people, the ones still with us, anyway. I should be able to set up meetings for them if you let me know when it's convenient for you."

"That is great news, Dewi. Well done. As for Hefin Thomas, I may find out more about him from the three I *can* see, and take it from there. To be honest, I wasn't sure whether you'd be able to locate all of them that quickly, so great job."

"What about them coffees then?" Dewi grinned.

"Blimey, you drive a hard bargain, Hughes."

9

A CHOICE OF THERAPISTS

George Langley had aged well.

He appeared agile for seventy-one as he crossed the room to pick up a spare chair and bring it forward for Yvonne.

She thanked him, feeling awkward that she hadn't fetched it for herself.

"Sorry," he apologised. "We had a guest speaker over last night, introducing a novel technique. We had to rearrange the furniture. I haven't got around to putting it back."

His full head of hair was white, in contrast with the old photograph she had seen. He had kept himself in shape. There was no spare flesh anywhere. The lines in his skin gave him an air of knowledgeability. He had dressed in corduroy trousers, shirt and tie. A tweed jacket hung over the back of a chair on the far side of the room.

"This isn't a treatment room, then?" Yvonne asked, even though she could clearly see that it wasn't, there being no bed, chair, or chaise. A long table surrounded by chairs took up the middle space, and a large window to the outside made up most of one wall.

"No." Langley shook his head. "This is the meeting room for staff and guests. We have three treatment rooms, they are the other side of the corridor."

Yvonne nodded. "I see. How long have you had your clinic here?"

"Oh, let me see, around thirty years. We set it up in the late eighties. Eighty-seven, I think it was. Myself and Brian have been here ever since. We have other practitioners to help, from time-to-time as and when it's necessary, which isn't that often. They usually come from out of area."

"Have you always called on outside help when things get busy?"

"Not always, only since we expanded our client base in two-thousand-and-one."

"I see. How many clients do you have?"

"We currently have around fifty active cases, but this can fluctuate between thirty and a hundred-and-fifty cases. Hence the need to take on extra practitioners occasionally."

"I see. Who pays for the treatment? The clients?"

George cleared his throat. "Some do, yes. Private and overseas patients always pay, though sometimes that is through insurance. Some patients can get treatment on the NHS, depending on the condition. Some NHS patients are expected to pay, however."

Yvonne was busy making notes. "Do you have many clients who wish to stop smoking?"

Langley nodded. "A significant number want help with stopping smoking. That, and anxiety and depression disorders, comprise are largest proportion of cases."

"I see. Mr Langley, have you got patient records going back to nineteen-ninety?"

"Nineteen-ninety?" He looked at her open-mouthed. "Why do you ask?"

"I'm curious."

"Not that far, no, we don't. We only hold records for up to ten years. Originally, we kept records for longer, but data protection stopped all that."

The DI pursed her lips. "So, if I were to request records for nineteen-ninety, you are saying you couldn't supply them?"

"That's exactly what I am saying."

"I see." Yvonne sat up straight in her chair, looking George Langley directly in the eye. "Mr Langley, does the name Sheila Winters mean anything to you?"

He screwed his face up. "Sheila Winters? Erm, no. No, it doesn't I'm afraid."

"Are you sure?" The DI pressed her lips into a thin line, pen paused over her pad.

"I'm sure the name doesn't ring a bell."

"What if I added the year nineteen-ninety, would it make any difference?"

He shook his head, shifting in his seat. "No, still nothing, I'm afraid."

"Very well. It was a long time ago, I guess it would be difficult to recall, without records, anyway."

Langley nodded. "We have seen so many people over the years. Unless they have some distinguishing feature, lots of people get lost in the crowds."

There was something about the way he said it. It made the DI uncomfortable. People were paying money, perhaps a lot of money, telling him their deepest secrets. It seemed to mean little to the man before her. But then, it was a business, and they had a large client base. Perhaps, as long as the patients got the required outcomes, that was all that mattered. It still didn't sit right with her. She felt that she would remember clients and all their stories. Maybe, she sighed, she was deluding herself.

"Is that all, Inspector?" Langley asked. He smiled, but his eyes remained cool as they scrutinised her face.

Yvonne sensed he was anxious about something. She nodded. "For now. I was hoping to speak to your business partner, though, Brian Watson?"

"Ah, yes, Brian. He's out, I'm afraid. Won't be back until this afternoon."

"I see. He works part time, doesn't he? Would it be convenient to return later today?" She asked, picking up her coat from the back of her chair.

"I'd have to ask him." He cleared his throat. "Why don't you call us, say, two o'clock?"

The DI nodded. "Fine. I'll call you at two. Thank you for your time."

He held the door open for her. "It's a pleasure, Inspector."

ALTHOUGH EQUAL PARTNERS with George Langley, Brian Watson was almost ten years his junior at sixty-four.

Just like George, Brian had kept himself in shape, though he had fared less well in the hair department, having lost all but a ring of hair that ran from just above one ear, around to the other, in contrast with the long brown locks he had sported in the photograph from nineteen-ninety.

He had the same smart-casual feel to his dress, however, wearing a shirt and jumper with jeans. He no longer wore a neckerchief.

"Thank you for seeing me, Mr Watson."

"Call me Brian." He held out his hand, giving her a broad smile. "And it's a pleasure." A smile lit his eyes.

She couldn't help smiling back. "How long have you guys had your clinic here on the industrial estate?" she asked. George Langley had already told her, but it was a good lead question, and it didn't hurt to compare and contrast their answers.

"Three decades, give or take. A long time, anyhow. Sometimes I ask myself why I have stayed in one place for so long. But, the fact is, I like it around here. It's scenic, I have everything I need, and my youngest is studying here at the university. My ex-wife is here, too. We are still good friends, all of which make it less likely that I'll ever move elsewhere."

"Of course." Yvonne nodded. "I understand you work part time?"

"I do. Well, mostly I do. I am nominally three days a week. I often work way over that, however. I find it hard to say no to people and, even more so, to George. He has been an understanding colleague over the years."

"How long have you and George known each other?"

He laughed, leaning back in his chair. "Oh, George and I, we go way back. We were best friends in school. Always up to mischief together, always in trouble together, and always standing outside of the headmaster's office together. He was the instigator, of course." He laughed again.

"It must be fun, being able to work with your best friend."

"Oh, it is. Well, mostly. We have the occasional argument about practice, you know. We sometimes prefer a different approach. Those are usually fairly minor disagreements. Otherwise, we still get on like a house on fire. He was best man at both of my weddings."

Yvonne tapped her pen against her chin. "Mr Watson, if I said the name Sheila Winters to you, would it mean anything?"

He frowned. "Sheila Winters... Sheila Winters... There's something familiar about that name. Winters." He screwed his face up. "Wait, wasn't she the lady who lost more memory than intended?" It was a rhetorical question. His eyes flicked from side-to-side as he looked at the ceiling.

"What do you mean, more memory than intended?"

He brought his gaze back to her. "There was a case, years ago. They mentioned it at a local hypnosis therapy convention. A conference, if you will. A case of a lady who had undergone a modified technique to change a behaviour. Could have been smoking? And, to reduce the chance of her returning to the habit, they altered her memory such that she wouldn't remember having the habit or even having the treatment for it. I think her name was Winters, but I didn't find that out right away. They anonymised her case for the purposes of the conference, but practitioners were discussing it afterwards because she was local. I am almost sure the name was Winters. And, when you say Sheila Winters, that definitely rings a bell."

Yvonne leaned forward in her chair, her eyes fixed on Watson. "How much memory did she lose?"

"She wasn't able to recognise some people she knew. Parts of her recent history had gone. She appeared to have lost months, altogether. The local medical practice were asking serious questions about her hypnotherapy treatment."

"I see. Who was her therapist?"

Brian shook his head. "I don't recall. I am not sure I ever knew. Hang on, I'll go ask George. Do you mind?" he asked, rising from his chair.

Yvonne shook her head. "No, I don't mind. Please, go ahead."

"I'll be right back," he called as he headed for the door.

The DI thought about Sheila Winters, and how frightened and confused she must have been when she realised she had lost parts of her memory. She imagined it took a great deal of trust to place your mind in the control of another. You had to hope your trust was well-placed and that they would treat you with the utmost care. Something had clearly gone wrong for Mrs Winters.

"I'm afraid George doesn't recall," Watson announced as he rejoined her. "He was struggling to even remember her case being mentioned at the convention. And, to be honest, I could have the wrong person entirely. If so, I apologise."

Yvonne held up a hand. "No problem, don't worry. Thank you for asking him for me."

He smiled, but there was an edge to it. It didn't have the warmth of earlier.

The DI wondered whether the two men had agreed to keep quiet. Radio silence. "How easy is it to influence another person hypnotically?" she asked, tilting her head.

"Can you remember the last time you drove your car?"

"Yes."

"Can you remember the route you took?"

"Yes."

"Start recalling it, from the time you switched on your engine, though every mile along the way. See the scenery, the road, the road markings appearing from under the car in front."

"Okay..." Yvonne was seeing the first two miles of the journey from Newtown police station to Aberystwyth.

"If you continued, you would likely go into trance. While

your conscious mind is pre-occupied with visualising, I could speak directly to your subconscious."

Yvonne snapped to attention, more than a little worried that she would be unduly influenced. She straightened her skirt.

Brian Watson grinned. "It's easier than you think."

"I see. Have you come across poor practice?"

"I haven't. Not really, I think even in the example I remembered from the convention, it was more a case of accidental harm than deliberate malpractice."

"I see."

"I think most, if not all, practitioners want the best outcomes for their patients and the results really can be astounding. People's lives transformed. Hypnosis is powerful."

"I can see how it would be."

"You've never tried it yourself, then?" He tilted his head, mirroring her.

"No, never. You have a soothing voice." The words spilled out before she could stop them. She felt awkward.

"It has been said." He smiled. "Is that everything, Inspector?"

"Yes." Yvonne stood up, extending her hand, brushing hair from her face to hide the colour which had risen in her cheeks. "Mr Watson, thank you for your time. You've been very helpful." She gave him her card. "Please call me if you remember any more about Sheila Winters' memory loss."

Watson read her card before placing it in his wallet. "I will, Inspector Yvonne Giles."

∾

Simon Hopkins had agreed to meet her at Starbucks cafe at the top of Great Darkgate Street, Aberystwyth.

The DI sat, sipping a Latte, and watching the rain through the window as he arrived, shaking his umbrella before coming in. He had told her she could expect to see him with a red one, like he was meeting her after picking her up on some dating site.

She waved.

He deposited his mac on the back of the seat opposite and held out his hand.

Yvonne stood to shake it.

"So you are Inspector Giles." His eyes twinkled. At sixty-seven, he had a lived-in countenance, and a confident air that said he had seen a lot in life and could deal with most things.

"I am." She returned his smile. "But call me Yvonne, by all means."

"And you must call me Simon." He grinned. "Would you like another coffee, Yvonne? What are you having?"

She came out from behind the table. "No, I'm getting these, what will it be?"

Simon shook his head. "I cannot allow a lady to buy me coffee," he said, blocking her path.

The DI sidestepped him. "Why ever not?" She smiled to avoid giving offence. "What did you say you wanted?"

"An americano, please," he acquiesced, clearing his throat, his face tense.

"Coming right up," Yvonne suppressed a grin.

When she returned, Hopkins was watching a couple having an argument in the street outside. The guy stormed off. "Oh dear," he said. "That guy should be a hypnotherapist. He'd be able to control her better."

"Sorry?" She frowned at him, shocked at his bold assertion.

He flicked her a glance, looking like he wanted to say something else, but thought better of it. "I just think it's a shame they are fighting like that. There's no need."

"I'm sure they'll make it up." Yvonne set the coffees down on the table, pushing his americano towards him.

"Thank you." He raised his eyes to hers. "You said you'd like to talk about a historic case?"

The DI grimaced. "I don't know that it is one of yours. I'm afraid I am not at all sure whose case it was. But I am hoping you might know something about it or be able to tell me who the practitioner was?"

"Okay..." His eyes narrowed. "So, who are we talking about?"

Yvonne lowered her voice, leaning in. "Her name was Sheila Winters and the year would have been nineteen-ninety."

"Sheila Winters," he repeated. "Nineteen-ninety... Nope, not ringing any bells with me. Can you tell me any more?"

"They discussed her case at a hypnotherapy convention in the early nineties. Apparently, she suffered memory loss that could have related to her treatment. I believe they intended some memory loss, in that she wasn't to remember being a smoker, or of having treatment for it. However, it seems she lost more of her memory and, I'm told, it was a hot topic of conversation between therapists at the convention."

"Now you say that, I do vaguely remember a case like that being discussed at a conference. It was a female case, too. I'm afraid I cannot confirm the name, though. I'm not sure I ever knew it. What I can say, however, is that the rumour was that it was Hefin Thomas's case. He was a hypnotherapist working in the area. He's dead now, poor bloke. Died of heart failure several years back. But I am sure it was his case they were discussing."

"But, you cannot confirm it was Shelia Winters?"

He shook his head. "I'm afraid I can't."

"Did they say how she had lost more memory than she should?"

"I think they felt it was accidental although there was talk, if I remember rightly, of her possibly having received a head injury."

The DI tilted her head, narrowing her eyes. "A head injury?"

"Yes."

"Was there any evidence of a head injury? Did she have an accident around that time?"

"I don't know that there was any evidence apart from her having suffered hair loss from the back of her head. A relatively small patch, however, and there was nothing to confirm it was from an injury."

"Was there a cut or a bruise in the bald patch?"

"I don't think so. By the time the memory loss came to her therapist's attention, any wound would have healed anyway, I'm guessing. At any rate, I think it was just a bald patch, and they found no definite link to a head injury. They assessed her, I believe, at a neuropsychology clinic and her general cognitive function was fine. She had simply lost a portion of her recent memory."

"Still, it must have been frightening for her."

"Oh, I'm sure it was. I would have thought Hefin would have reassured her, though. He had an excellent manner with his patients. He was a decent bloke."

Yvonne sipped her coffee, leaning back in her chair. "I

understand you work online a lot these days. It makes perfect sense in this day and age." She studied his face.

"Yes, I take on new clients through my website and can work with them one-to-one online. It works very well. It saves on travel time, too. I am paid per session, or per course, and I do all my advertising online. I sometimes do consultancy work locally and elsewhere in the UK, but I would say that seventy percent of my work is now on the net."

"I see. No plans to retire then?"

He shook his head. "I am not ready to be put out to pasture yet, Yvonne."

"I didn't mean-"

He laughed. "It's okay, you're right. I probably should start taking it easy, but I enjoy what I do and, at sixty-seven, I feel I can do it for a few years yet."

"I admire your dedication." She smiled. "And, I am in agreement. I love my job. I think they will need to force me out when they decide it is time for me to retire."

"Then you know where I'm coming from. Oh, no..." He looked through the window. "In the words of Annie Lennox, here comes the rain again."

Yvonne turned to see. "Wow, it really is stair rods."

"Yes." Hopkins rode from his seat. "I think that means another round of coffee."

YVONNE POURED over the photographs back in the station. If Simon Hopkins was right, Hefin Thomas had been Sheila Winter's hypnotherapist. She took out the picture of him in his flat cap, intending to show it to Sheila again. Perhaps, when viewing it in isolation, she might remember something.

The DI knew the least about Hefin and would have to pick people's brains to find out who he really was. Simon Hopkins had said he had a good bedside manner. He would certainly have had his clients' trust.

She wondered if he still had family living in the area and jotted down a reminder to find out.

She checked the clock. Five-thirty. Time to make tracks back to Newtown.

JUST ABOUT TO LEAVE ABERYSTWYTH STATION, HER phone rang.

She pulled it from her coat pocket. "Yvonne Giles."

"Detective Giles?"

"Yes."

"It's Sheila Winters."

"Sheila, hello, what can I do for you?"

Sheila took a deep breath. "I've remembered the wood. I know where it is. It's up a long, windy lane, off the road to Borth."

"Really? What's it called?"

"Black Wood. It's on private land."

"Who owns the land?"

"A farmer, I think."

"Look, this is fantastic news." Yvonne ran a hand through her hair. "How did you remember the where it was?"

"I fell asleep this afternoon. When I woke, I had this lucid memory of walking along the lane and seeing the sign.

It was a roughly painted name, on wood about twelve-by-twelve inches. The letters were in purple paint, I think."

"Well, that is something we should be able to find, if it's still there. If not, we might find someone who could corroborate its previous existence."

"Exactly." Sheila's voice shook. "Although, I was really hoping that the murder was a false memory. If we find Black Wood and the sign, I can no longer cling to that hope."

Yvonne grimaced on the other end of the phone. "Look, even if the wood and sign exist, given the fragile state of your memory, we still won't know whether a murder actually took place. We can't be sure what you witnessed or what your memories mean, yet. But this is something tangible that we can check."

"Could we go tomorrow?" There was a pleading in Sheila's voice. The DI could almost hear her biting her lip.

Yvonne thought about Tasha and sighed. Their weekends together were precious. but this had to take precedence. "Yes, yes, all right. We'll meet tomorrow and explore the lane to Black Wood."

10

THE REMAINS OF BLACK WOOD

Yvonne parked her car in a tiny dirt lay-by, doing her best to keep the wheels clear of the deep mud ruts left by a tractor.

Switching off the engine, she could already hear the chatter of birds and the cawing of crows. A buzzard soared high in the cold, cloudless sky.

"Come on," she said to Sheila Winters. "Let's go."

Sheila didn't move right away, but stared ahead through the windscreen, her eyes wide.

"Are you all right?" Yvonne asked. "We don't have to do this now, if you don't want to."

Sheila snapped back to her as though returning from a trance. "This is the right place," she said. "It started here."

"Are you okay to go ahead?" The DI enquired, her voice soft.

Sheila nodded, though her hand shook as she reached for the door handle.

"We'll take it slowly. If you feel the need to turn back, tell me and we'll stop, okay?" She squeezed Sheila's arm, giving her a reassuring smile.

Sheila nodded. "I'm ready."

Yvonne shouldered a small backpack, and they set off up the lane, leaving behind them the noise of main road traffic.

She stayed a pace behind Sheila, such that she would not be influencing Sheila's advance. The DI wanted Sheila's recall and instinct to be the only guides, though she took out a local ordinance map from her coat pocket to check their rough location. They were close to Black Wood. They were on the right track. All she needed to do was follow.

The lane was narrow, about three-people deep, with hedges either side. Wheels had compacted stone and mud either side of a central line of grass which tracked the entire length.

Further along, the hedges disappeared, replaced by mesh fencing and the occasional stile. Open fields became trees, sparse trees became more densely packed, and the mesh fencing finally ended.

"This is it. This is Black Wood." Sheila stopped walking, her gaze casting around.

The DI could see that Mrs Winters' eyes were unfocussed. She was seeing another time and place.

Yvonne kept her voice low. "Where's the sign, Sheila? Are we close to it?"

Sheila nodded, her head drifting.

"Can you take us to it?"

"Yes."

They walked a further two hundred yards before Sheila deviated to the left. "Here. The sign was here."

"Are you sure? I don't see anything." Yvonne scoured the ground. "It probably disappeared a long time ago."

Sheila frowned, spinning slowly around.

The DI could tell she was back in the present. "Where did you go from here, Sheila?"

"I'm hungry," was the answer.

Yvonne took the backpack off her shoulder, reaching inside for sandwiches wrapped in foil. "Here," she said, holding the open package to Sheila. "Have one of these. Cheese and onion, I made them this morning."

"Thanks." Sheila took a triangle and munched on it, her head tilted in thought.

The DI packed the rest away.

"Let's keep going. We're close, I know we are." Mrs Winters continued along the forest road.

They had walked another thousand yards when Sheila stopped, her whole body shaking.

"What is it?" Yvonne asked, placing a hand on her upper arm.

A shiny layer of sweat had developed on Sheila's forehead.

"Sheila?"

"It's through there." She pointed through the trees to a small clearing containing small mounds of forest debris. Tears hovered along her lower eyelids.

"Are you okay to go on?" Yvonne asked.

"The hut was in there."

Yvonne cast her eyes around the clearing. There didn't appear to be any sort of structure. "Do you want to wait here while I check it out?" she asked the still-shaking Mrs Winters.

Sheila shook her head. "I'll come with you."

They walked together, taking their time, stepping gingerly over and around the dead branches and other detritus.

In the middle of the clearing, Sheila pointed to the ground, tears streaming down her face. "It was here." She twirled around, looking at the surrounding trees. "I had the axe in my hand. I knew what I had to do. I was so upset, angry and afraid."

"What were you angry about? Why were you afraid?"

"I don't know. There's a fog about it. A thick fog in my brain. I see the shack, but it's blurred. My mind is focussed but, at the same time, confused. I only know I have to break in there. Break in and kill the creature inside."

"So, you go to the door of the shack?" Yvonne stared at Mrs Winters' tear-stained face. Sheila's eyes remained unfocussed.

"Yes. I can't get it open. It's locked or stiff. I smashed at the handle with the axe, and then at the lock. The door smashes open." Sheila sobbed, her face soaked, strings of saliva formed between her lips. Mucous ran from her nose. "She begged me."

"Begged you to stop?"

"Begged me not to hurt her."

"Do you know why you wanted hurt her. Did you think she had done something to you?"

Sheila shook her head. "I don't know. I brought the axe down. Blood went everywhere. I couldn't stop. I carried on smashing it down."

"Okay, okay, stop." Yvonne did not want Sheila to suffer unnecessarily. "Can you remember what happened afterwards?"

Sheila closed her eyes, hands to her head, her fingers in her hair. "I had a shovel." She strolled to the opposite edge of the clearing, followed by the DI. "I think it's through here."

"What's through there?"

"The grave. I had a shovel," She repeated. "I took the shovel through here."

"What about the body? Where was the body?"

Sheila shook her head. "I don't know."

"Did you carry the body? Did you drag it?"

"No. No, I don't remember."

"It's okay. You have the shovel in your hand. What happens now?"

"I'm hot. Sweating. There's a noise in my ears."

"Noise? What noise?"

"High-pitched ringing."

"Like tinnitus?"

"Yes. I feel thirsty."

Yvonne reached into her backpack for a bottle of water. She held it out to Sheila, who pushed it away.

"This way." Mrs Winter set off again, picking her way through the trees.

Yvonne followed, but threw a look behind her, making sure she knew their way back to the car. Her stomach muscles clenched tight. Sweat developed on her upper lip. She felt uneasy in the forest with this woman she barely knew.

They came to another clearing. Smaller, this time, but the floor had similar forest detritus.

"I know it's here, somewhere."

Yvonne frowned. "What's here? The body?"

"I was so tired. I didn't want to dig. I stopped, I don't think it was deep enough."

"The grave?" Yvonne asked, keeping her voice low.

"I should have dug it deeper, but I couldn't."

"Did you want it to be deeper? Did someone else tell you it should be deeper?"

Sheila shook her head, her eyes wide open and staring. "I don't know."

"Was the body there?"

"It was next to me. I was digging, and it was next to me."

"What happened next?"

"I rolled it in. I pushed the mud over it. It wasn't good enough."

"Who thought it wasn't good enough?"

Sheila ignored her. "I got leaves and branches. I put them on the top. It scared me. I wanted to climb in with the girl."

"Where were you?"

Sheila walked to the edge of the clearing, pointing to the ground. "I think it was here."

Yvonne peered at branches and mud. A small stream had gouged a narrow corridor through. "You're sure it's here?"

Sheila nodded.

Yvonne bent to clear branches and other debris, kicking back stones and toe-poking the earth. As she kicked at it, part of the mud bank gave way, toppling into the stream. The DI grabbed a large stick and poked at it, breaking away more of the thick dirt.

Then she saw it. A stained, rounded object. A lump developed in her throat as she gingerly scratched away more of the surrounding dirt. As more of the object became clear, Yvonne fell back. A mud-filled eye socket stared back at her.

Heart thumping, she turned to Sheila. "Sheila Winters. I am arresting you on suspicion of murder. You do not have to say anything, but it may harm your defence if you do not mention, when questioned, something you later rely on in court. Anything you do say can be taken down in evidence."

"I'm sorry." Sheila sobbed. "I'm so sorry."

Yvonne telephoned DCI Llewelyn, to inform him of the development, and to let him coordinate the response. She then took Sheila Winters by the arm, escorting her to the car. "Do I need to handcuff you?" she asked.

Sheila shook her head.

There was no resistance in her detainee. Yvonne led her back to the car.

"ARE YOU OKAY? Where's your murderess?" DCI Llewelyn asked when she called him from Aberystwyth station.

"She's in the cells. A solicitor is with her."

"Well done, catching a murderer single-handed."

"I didn't exactly catch her, sir. She came to me. And I am not entirely sure she is wholly responsible."

The DCI sighed, "Yvonne, you're the only person I know who can talk themselves out of having done a good job."

"Something doesn't sit right, Chris. There's a lot more to this story, I know there is."

"What do you mean, it doesn't sit right?"

"Well, she remembers committing the murder, she remembers being angry, upset, and afraid, but she can't tell me why. She doesn't have a rationale."

"Maybe she hasn't remembered it yet?"

Yvonne sighed. "Well, that's the other thing. Her memories of the murder are hazy, she tells me. Like, she wasn't in her normal mind when she committed it."

"If she was feeling strong emotion, that could be the reason. You know, the red mist and all that?"

"But, again, she remembers digging a hole and burying the body, but not getting the body to the burial site. It is difficult terrain. It's uneven. There are large tree roots and small watercourses. The burial site is several hundred yards from the place she thinks she killed someone. I don't believe she could have moved the body, to where it is, without help. Perhaps, she didn't move it at all."

"What do you mean?"

"I mean, someone could have been influencing her. I believe that person may have been her hypnotherapist."

"I see. Not an open-and-shut case, then?"

"I don't believe so, sir."

"So, what do you intend doing next?"

"I've identified her therapist from thirty years ago."

"Well, that's something."

"Except, he's deceased." She grimaced, moving the phone from her ear.

"Oh."

She put the phone back to her ear. "I'm disappointed to say the least, but I am investigating with other therapists in the area and I could still get answers."

"Are you sure you're not complicating this unnecessarily?"

"Maybe I am, but I wouldn't be doing my job properly if I didn't follow this up. Do you know if SOCO are at the scene?"

"They are on their way, and uniform are getting a search team together, to go over that part of the wood."

"That is good news. Thank you, sir. Sheila Winters will need rest after she has consulted with her solicitor. I will speak with her tomorrow. What I say will depend on what SOCO find. I expect we'll formally charge her sometime this week, or early next."

"Very well." Llewellyn cleared his throat. "We'll await the SOCO and search team reports before deciding on the next step. In the meantime, it sounds like you have some therapists to talk to."

"Thank you, sir."

As the DI ended the call, she couldn't help feeling for Sheila in the cells. She would be terrified, confused and riddled with guilt. Yvonne could only imagine how it might feel to wake up one morning with memories of an event you didn't even know had taken place, let alone one so shocking. Talk about life throwing a curve ball.

YVONNE WAS HARD AT WORK, typing up her statement from the day before. She had gone to work early, expecting to hear news from the search teams.

Dewi strode over to her desk. "Ma'am, you should get yourself to Aberystwyth."

"Really? Why?" She scrutinised Dewi's face. He looked pale.

"They've found more remains in Black Wood. They think they are at least four or five bodies, Yvonne."

She sat back in her chair, pushing her glasses atop her head. She stared at him, wide-eyed. "Oh, my God."

"Your Mrs Winters has been a very busy girl-"

"She's not my Mrs Winters, Dewi, and... It can't be her. The idea is... It's just ridiculous. No, it's preposterous. She couldn't have been responsible for multiple deaths."

Dewi grinned. "Something gives me the feeling you don't think she did it, ma'am."

She shot him a look, then grinned despite herself. "Cheeky beggar. And no, I don't think she is responsible for so many bodies. *If* the deaths are linked, and we are dealing with a serial killer, I don't think that killer would have been twenty-year-old Sheila Winters. I'll put my neck on the line and say that someone or something else is behind this. A puppet master, if you will. I think Sheila got involved in something beyond her control. Was she made to kill another girl just like her? I don't know. I am still getting my head around it all but, I have a feeling that it involved hypnosis. If Sheila killed several girls, I think someone else made her. However, I want to reassure you that I *am* keeping an open mind, really I am. Let's see where the forensic evidence leads."

Dewi nodded. "I should think the DCI won't object to you heading up an MIT to investigate this, now there are actual bodies."

"I hope so, Dewi. Fancy joining me?"

Dewi placed his hands on his hips. "Try to stop me."

11

THE UNIDENTIFIED

An hour later, and they were suiting-up outside of the cordon surrounding the half-acre of woodland containing the remains.

The sky looked black enough for a downpour, but had so far delivered only a drizzle. The DI hoped it wouldn't change its mind.

SOCO worked in teams of two per set of remains.

Hazmat suits on, Yvonne and Dewi entered the cordon and approached the first of the tents where one team was engaged. It was where the DI had found the first skull.

"What have we got?" she asked, adjusting her mask.

"This one looks to be female, late teens or early twenties."

Yvonne pressed her lips hard together.

The male SOCO officer continued. "Someone hacked her with a sharp, heavy implement, most likely an axe."

"Before or after death?" The DI asked, although she knew from Sheila Winters' account it was likely to be the former.

"Can't say for sure, but probably prior to death. You

should check with the pathologist after he has had a good look at the bones."

Yvonne nodded. "Of course."

"It was a shallow grave, not more than a couple of feet deep. Someone must have run out of steam."

"I'm surprised it took so long for anyone to discover the body. Surely, a dog would have found it? The smell of a rotting corpse is hard to miss. "

He shrugged. "It's a bit out of the way. We're miles from the major centres. I doubt anyone comes this far to walk their dogs."

"I guess that's why the killer chose this place." She sighed, eyes scanning the trees.

"The gaffer says you have someone in custody for it." His knees clicked as he stood, arching his back to relieve the stiffness.

"Wow." She raised an eyebrow. "News travels fast. Our guest is only *one* of our persons of interest. There will be others."

His assertion had grated with her. It was a reminder of how easily rumours took off and of how serious was the responsibility of police when arresting for murder. Mud stuck, even when the person proved culpably innocent as could happen with Sheila Winters.

She was about to say something along these lines, when someone else caught her attention. It was Steve Besson. She had met him only once before, but she recognised the thirty-seven-year-old pathologist from Ceredigion. The DI made her way over to him, followed by her sergeant.

"Steve." She extended her hand. "Hi. Yvonne Giles. We met-"

"Ah, Yvonne. Nice to see you again." He moved his mask lower so he could talk more easily. "Not a pretty site, this."

"No." She shook her head. "Can I ask, are they all female?"

He nodded. "They are. And, from what I can tell, they were all young when they died. I'll include the ages in my report obviously, but I believe there were none older than early twenties."

"Do all the remains show injuries consistent with an axe?"

He shook his head. "No. As far as I can tell, only two of them have axe marks. Another has markings more consistent with a knife. And the others, I can't say until we've got the bones properly cleaned up and had a better look at them. One thing is for sure, we will have to run dental comparisons and possibly facial reconstructions to find out who they were."

"Yes." Yvonne wiped at the rain on her brow with her plastic sleeve. It didn't help. "We'll get on with MisPer lists for comparison. We have one or two names already. At least some families will now get closure, such as it is."

"Yes." He gave her the look that said, 'I'm sorry, I've really got to get on.'

She stepped back, giving him a smile. "Thank you. I'll catch up with you in a day or two."

"Great." He nodded and crossed to a tent where a SOCO officer was motioning to him.

"I'M NOT responsible for more than one victim, am I?" Sheila stared, wide-eyed, her head flailing around. "There are no other girls in my flashbacks. None. Only one girl. Just one. I swear I didn't hurt any others."

"I understand." Yvonne nodded. "I had to ask the question."

"How many were there?" Sheila sat back, becoming still.

"Five, so far."

"So far? Oh, God. Do you think there's more?"

"I don't know. I hope not. The search teams are still out looking."

"I hope there's no more, too." Sheila's eyes were on the table.

"Are you sure you see the same girl in every flashback?"

"Yes."

"If you saw her photograph, could you identify her?"

Sheila nibbled her lip. "I don't know. Maybe."

"If you're not sure you could identify her, what makes you so sure it's the same girl."

"I can't tell you. I just know."

"Do you know the identity of the girl? Are you hearing a name or thinking of one in any of your memories?"

Sheila shook her head.

"I can show you images of missing girls from the time. See if you recognise any."

Sheila nodded.

Yvonne pursed her lips, her hands together, propping up her chin. "Is it only an axe that you see in your flashbacks? Do you see anything else? Any other weapons?"

Sheila's brow creased. "It's just an axe. I'm holding it in both hands. I have nothing else on me."

"Can you tell me what you are wearing? Can you see your clothing in these flashbacks?"

Sheila shook her head. "Not really. When I look down at the axe, I get the impression of the colour blue. A blue skirt, maybe? Jeans? I don't know. I get more idea of my emotions and the surroundings than anything else. I'm sorry, I am not being much help, am I? I don't know why I would have killed one girl, let alone five. Except, obviously, I believe I murdered one of them. That's why I am here."

"Of course."

"Will you charge me?" Sheila tilted her head, tears in her eyes.

"I don't know. Not yet, at least." Yvonne rubbed her chin.

"Why? I have confessed. I showed you were the body was. You've arrested me on suspicion."

"I know. But first, we are relying on memories, which you said are hazy. Second, we have no corroborating evidence. We may get confirmation from forensics but, until we do, we don't know whether someone was exerting undue influence over you. Plus, you only remember one murder when we have five. Have you had any further memories involving your hypnotherapist?"

Sheila shook her head. "I am still seeing him only in outline. Like a silhouette. That and hearing his voice. That's it."

Yvonne pulled Hefin Thomas' photograph out from under her papers and pushed it towards her. "Who is this? Do you recognise him?"

Sheila fingered the photograph, like a blind person might examine Braille. "He looks familiar. I think I've seen him somewhere. I don't know where. Who is he?"

The DI thought about telling her but, afraid of implanting memory, she instead withdrew the photo and changed the subject. "Are you hungry? And would you like a cup of tea? Your solicitor is on his way."

"I'd love some food and a cuppa." Sheila smiled. "Thank you."

12

BELONGINGS

"They found clothing with some remains, ma'am." Dewi passed her a mug of hot tea. "It seems the girls had their clothing tossed into their graves after them."

"So they were naked when buried? The motive may have been sexual. I wonder why they buried the clothing with the girls? Somebody clearly thought they had found a good hiding place, they had no fear of the bodies being found and identified."

"Seems that way, doesn't it?" Dewi agreed.

"I will ask the male hypnotists to record a few lines each from a hypnotherapy session for me."

"Why? What are you thinking?" Dewi tilted his head.

"Sheila still cannot visualise her therapist. However, she tells me she can hear his voice. I'd like to have her listen to their voices and see if she recognises one of them."

Dewi frowned. "I thought you told me her therapist was Hefin Thomas, and that he had passed away."

"He did. And, if he was the person Sheila remembers, she won't recognise any of the voices."

"What are you up to?" Dewi pursed his lips? "Do you think someone other than her therapist was influencing her? Another therapist?"

"I'll tell you when I have thought things through," Yvonne said, tapping her nose.

"Fair enough." Dewi shrugged. "The DCI wants to see you, anyway. Apparently he is having a nightmare with the press."

The DI nodded. "I know. They are everywhere, but you can hardly blame them. It's not every day we find five sets of remains in a forest. I'll go see him when I've finished this brew. Thank you, Dewi." She raised her mug to him.

"You're welcome, Yvonne."

"Oh, one more thing..."

"Ma'am?"

"Can you find out what cars each of our therapists owned in nineteen-ninety? Specifically, I'd be interested if any of them had a small mustard-coloured car."

"Will do." Dewi nodded, returning to his desk.

"COME IN." The DCI had his glasses on, scanning through several sheafs of paper on his desk. "Ah, Yvonne, sit down. I've been meaning to get to you."

"Dewi said you wanted to see me? I hear the press is being a nuisance."

Llewelyn sighed. "Reporters are literally following me everywhere. Honestly, I bet one of them would hold the loo roll for me in the toilet, if I asked them too."

The DI giggled at the thought.

"It's not funny, Yvonne. It's taking me twice as long to get anywhere, and I feel like I am the person who knows the least about what is happening with the case."

"That's because you left me on my own with it, sir."

He grunted. "Yes, I know, and I am sorry about that. However, we had very little to go on. I must say, you've done very well to get us to this point."

"Thank you, Sir."

"I understand you have arrested your suspect, and she's in custody. Mrs Winters?"

"Sheila Winters, yes. The court will probably grant her bail this morning, pending further questioning."

"You haven't charged her, then?"

Yvonne shook her head. "We don't have enough evidence for that. All we have, in fact, is her confession."

"I thought she led you to the bodies?"

"She took me to one body, yes. However, Sheila is adamant that she is not responsible for all five girls. She tells me she is certain she killed only one girl."

"So, you're saying she killed one of the victims and the others are there by coincidence?" He pulled a face.

"I don't think it was a coincidence, no. I believe someone else was behind these murders, including the one Sheila says she was responsible for. I have a feeling they influenced her into believing her victim was an evil entity that should be destroyed. I have a suspicion they did this using hypnosis or drugs."

"Could Mrs Winters have chosen to take illicit drugs and hallucinated? Talked herself into believing these women were evil?"

"Well, obviously, I can't rule that out. However, all the girls were naked when they were buried. That has me wondering whether there was a sexual motive. I am also wondering whether a predator might have convinced young women to murder each other."

"Could we be looking at a cult?"

"I don't know. I only know that Sheila Winters began having memories of the murder at the same time she had memories of having treatment with a male hypnotherapist. She knew nothing about either of those things for thirty years. The two may be linked. When Sheila is remembering the murder, she tells me the memories are hazy, as though she is in a trance as she approaches the hut, breaks into it, and murders the girl. I think we should explore that angle because it could be key."

Llewelyn nodded. "Very well. Keep me informed. Obviously, you will lead the cold case MIT, with myself as the public face and point of contact for reporters. Give me a list of the staff you think you'll need and I'll ensure you have them, within reason."

"Thank you, sir."

"Oh, and Yvonne?"

"Sir?"

"Please, don't do anything dangerous."

She held her hands up. "Who, Me?"

~

THAT EVENING, Yvonne travelled home to be with Tasha.

She needed the strength and reassurance of her partner's arms. For the entire journey, it was hard to shake images of young women, brutally murdered and left to rot in shallow graves. Not for the first time in her life, she wondered at the person who would do that. And this case felt more evil, because of the possibility that someone was pulling strings. That someone was causing women to kill each other.

She said this to Tasha as they sat together, in their pyjamas, after dinner. "Am I overthinking things?" She asked, leaning forward, her head in her hands. "Could it be that I just don't want to accept that Sheila, as a young woman, would have killed those girls by herself?"

Tasha tilted her head, her hand gently rubbing Yvonne's back. "No, I don't think you are overthinking it. Young women rarely commit those sorts of violent murders. There have been one-or-two famous occasions in the past, when women were involved in bloody murders. An example would be the killing of the heavily pregnant Sharon Tate, and her friends, committed by the cult followers of Charles Manson. Those girls were off their heads on drugs, however. They were in an altered mental state. Manson had indoctrinated them."

Yvonne nodded. "That's not unlike the scenario I'm proposing, if Sheila was in a hypnotic trance."

"I think it is entirely possible, given that she remembered killing someone at the same time she remembered being treated via hypnosis. In fact, I doubt remembering the two together is a coincidence. Have you identified her hypnotherapist?"

"I think so. His name was Hefin Thomas. He passed away a few years ago, so I cannot question him, but I can talk to those who knew him. Sheila hasn't recognised Hefin from his photograph, yet. I can't be sure whether she was his case until she does. But, if he was her therapist, we won't be able to prove his involvement unless we have a forensic miracle."

"Given the way this sort of recall progresses, Yvonne, Sheila's memory won't stop there. She'll get a lot more return to her over the coming weeks and months. You may have to be a little patient."

Yvonne grimaced. "The DCI will love that. He's literally fighting journalists on his lawn at the moment. He's taking the flack to protect me. I'm grateful to him."

Tasha scratched her head. "Has Sheila been psychologically assessed? Have the mental health team seen her at all?"

Yvonne shook her head. "Not yet. She has an appointment with a clinical psychologist next week. It's the earliest we could have an assessment done. She is out on bail in the meantime."

"I see."

"A community psychiatric nurse spoke with her at length and didn't deem her to be a risk. And, I have to say, I agree. She appears genuinely shocked and distressed at the memories. I think the trauma may have been a major factor in her memory loss."

"It wouldn't surprise me. Also, if she was being controlled via hypnosis, then it's possible they wiped her memory of the events. Her hypnotist could do that. Or, the loss could be due to a combination of trauma and hypnosis."

"I'm genuinely concerned for her. She will need a lot of support, going forward, if she is to move on. She appears trapped inside the memories at the moment. You can see in her eyes how tortured she is."

"I don't doubt it."

"What sort of person would manipulate others into doing such a thing?"

"Someone with an ego who enjoys power play. Perhaps, someone who would get sexual stimulation that way."

Yvonne turned her gaze to Tasha, her eyes flicking side-to-side. "The girls were naked. The killer had thrown their clothes into the graves after their bodies. A sexual motive is the obvious reason, and I think that would make Sheila far less likely to be the sole perpetrator."

"I agree. "

"If he was getting sexual stimulation, presumably he would have watched the whole thing?"

"Almost certainly, I would say."

"So he must have been there, in the shack."

Tasha nodded. "Or stood behind Sheila as she went in. Unless he was outside looking in through a window."

"I could ask Sheila about a window when I next see her. I'm a little concerned about planting false memories, though."

"Well, you could simply ask her if she noticed a window, and see what she says."

"I will, thanks."

"Are you working out of Aberystwyth station again?"

Yvonne nodded. "The incident room is there, so I will be running the cold case MIT from there. There'll be myself and Dewi, and the two Aberystwyth DCs, Sarah Evans and Ifan Hughes. Dai and Callum will help us, but only on a part-time basis, as they are also working a drug investigation in Newtown. I say heading up, but the DCI is the nominal head. This is inevitably attracting large amounts of news coverage and, like I said, he's going to take any flack. However, it will be myself running the day-to-day investigation, unless I need him."

"Sounds like a dream team." Tasha smiled. "Do you think you might need me?"

"If you're available, I would love you to join us." Yvonne pulled a face. "I'll maybe wait until the DCI is less hassled before asking him whether you can go on the payroll again."

"I would help you *for free* if you needed it, Yvonne, you realise that?"

"I know you would." Yvonne leaned in to kiss her partner on the lips. "That's because you are amazing."

As their kiss deepened, all conversation ended.

13

MORGUE

The five girls' skeletal remains lay on individual trollies in the morgue.

Their clothing remained with forensics for testing, but A4-sized photographs of the relevant items lay at the feet of each girl.

The DI took her time, going from trolley to trolley, picturing them as they might have been in life. She felt she owed them that much.

"We should know who some of them are within the next forty-eight hours, perhaps all of them, if they had dental treatment." Hanson handed her sheets detailing the injuries each girl had suffered, as evidenced by the markings on the bones. "If we can't identify them all that way, we'll move to digital reconstruction which will take around four days."

Yvonne had tasked Callum and Dai with cross-checking the items of clothing found with that worn by the young women who had disappeared from the area. Among those being checked were Tracy Merrifield and Susan Lee. To those names, Yvonne had added several missing girls from further afield. The DI hoped to have an idea who the girls were even before the results from dental records or facial reconstruction came in.

She turned to Hanson and nodded. "I understand. So, these are the injuries they suffered?" She scanned each girl's sheet.

"It's not a definitive list, Yvonne. There may have been wounds, including knife, axe, or blunt trauma injuries, that didn't leave marks on the bones but, given the frenzied nature of the attacks on the women, I would think there would be very few blows which did not impact the skeleton."

"I can't imagine what they went through." Yvonne pursed her lips, shaking her head. "It must have terrified them. I hope it ended quickly."

Hanson nodded. "Several had severe skull trauma. If those were the first blows, they wouldn't have known much about the rest of the attack."

"We'll be able to give some families closure, at least. Although, I never know whether that is a good thing. I don't know if I would prefer to imagine my loved one safe somewhere, living the high life, or know for certain they were dead. That someone had murdered them."

"It tears the loved ones apart, not knowing." Hanson ran his hand through his hair. "It wears them out. They can never stop waiting. Never stop looking."

Yvonne scrutinised Hanson's face. "Are you speaking from personal experience, Roger?" she asked, her voice soft.

His eyes were on the floor. "My father went out to work one morning and never came home. I was nine years old. Not a week goes by, even now, when I don't wonder what happened to him. We never found out."

"Oh God, Roger, I'm sorry..."

"Don't be. I learned to live with it a long time ago but, for years, we waited for him to telephone or to walk in through the front door."

"Did you have any idea what *might* have happened?"

"I blamed myself. I thought I'd been so naughty, he couldn't take it. I was so sure he had left because of me. I couldn't imagine him leaving because of my mother. He adored the ground she walked on."

"It wouldn't have been you."

"He was an engineer. He had worked in a team that developed engines for British warplanes."

"A clever man-"

"He had a locked box down in the garage. It's where he kept his best tools. After he disappeared, I searched everywhere for the key. I couldn't find it. I decided he must have kept it on the key ring with his house and car keys. He must have taken it with him."

"I see."

"For five years I didn't open it in case he came back. I felt like to do so would be to let him down. They were his private things. Then, one day, when I was fourteen, I took a crowbar and prized the lid. There were so many of his precious things in there. Plans, drawings, and some very expensive precision tools. The quality was amazing. I still use them today and they perform as well now as they did all those years ago."

"And he gave no sign he might leave?"

Hanson shook his head. "He didn't leave a note. His behaviour hadn't changed at all. I didn't see it coming and my mother... well, it devastated her. She never remarried. She saw dating anyone else as a kind of betrayal. My mother was convinced that something bad had happened to him, but she hoped he could sort it out and come home."

"I see."

"So, I think it is always better for the families to know what happened, even if it was something as horrendous as murder. It stops them blaming themselves or spending their whole lives endlessly searching."

"What was his name? Your dad, I mean."

"Milo."

"Milo?"

"My parents named him Milo because he was born in Milan. That hadn't been the plan. My grandparents had gone on holiday, and my dad came prematurely. So, Milo it was."

Yvonne placed a hand on Hanson's upper arm. "I hope you get closure before too long."

He smiled, though his eyes were sad. "Thank you."

YVONNE CAUGHT up with Dewi in the office. "How did you get on with clothing descriptions? Do we have any matches?"

Dewi scratched his head. "We might have mix-and-matches." He sighed. "*Some* items we found match items worn by *some* of the girls, but none of the sets of clothing that we found matches exactly with clothing being worn by any of the girls who disappeared."

The DI frowned. "So, what are we saying here? That the killer mixed all the garments up and threw them in with the girls afterwards?"

Dewi shook his head. "I don't know. It looks like the murderer might have jumbled them all up. And buried the clothes at a later date."

"What, opened the graves back up?"

Dewi shrugged. "Well, they were shallow enough for someone to do that."

"I see. Perhaps, wanting to cause further frustration for investigators." Yvonne sighed. "Well, in that case, we will have to wait for dental records and facial reconstructions. We've got no choice."

"Looks that way."

"Has anything come back from forensics regarding fibres, or DNA on the clothing? I know it's a long shot after all this time, but if he reopened the graves to bury clothes, he may have transferred material then, even if he didn't physically bury the bodies himself."

"True." Dewi nodded. "But he must have ferried the bodies to the burial sites, like you said, so he could have left material behind. With any luck, we'll find DNA from the girls who did the killing, and the person behind it all."

Yvonne crossed her fingers. "Let's hope."

"I'd better get on."

"There's one more thing, Dewi. Can you please set up an interview with the landowner? We'll talk to him together. I want to know what happened to the cabin where the murders took place. From Sheila's account, the walls and floor were drenched in blood. Someone must have cleaned that up. What was the shed used for, and what, if anything, did the landowner know? Also, who dismantled the cabin, and why?"

"Righty-oh, ma'am, I'll get onto it and set up a meeting for as soon as possible. I think uniform have taken a statement from the farmer. I'll see what he's said in it, so we'll be prepared."

"Excellent."

14

FLASHBACKS

Yvonne's mobile vibrated on her desk. "Yvonne Giles?"

"DI Giles? It's Susan Owen. You spoke to me the other day regarding a witness you said was having flashbacks."

"I did." The DI frowned in concentration.

"I saw the news... The bodies in the wood."

"Okay..." Yvonne wondered where this was going.

"A former patient has been in touch. I treated her for anxiety for several years."

"I see. Does she knows something about the remains in the wood?"

"She thinks she does, yes."

"What do you mean, she thinks?"

"She tells me she's been having strange memories that started around eighteen months ago. Flashbacks, if you will. She said she had dismissed them as nonsense but, when she saw the news reports from Black Wood, she began wondering if the memories could actually be real. She told me she thinks she might have been responsible for a girl's death, decades ago."

"Wow." Yvonne put a hand to her forehead as she processed this new information. "But she was *your* case?"

"Yes, mine."

"Not Hefin Thomas' case?"

"Sorry? I don't follow."

"Never mind. What's the woman's name, and can I speak with her?"

Susan cleared her throat on the other end of the line. "Her name is Pamela Mercer, and I don't know where she is. She hung up on me. I'm not sure why. I didn't have time to ask her where she is living and she either withheld her number, or telephoned from a network which doesn't allow the number to register."

"I see. Look, if she contacts you again, can you get a number that I can call her back on? In the meantime, I will see if our tech team can find out what the number was that called you. With your permission, we can contact your phone provider."

"You have my consent," Susan agreed. "I think you have my number?"

"I do, Susan, yes. Thank you."

"I'll be in touch." Susan hung up.

Yvonne scratched her head. Now there were two women possibly involved in murdering others. What an earth was she dealing with?

15

CABIN IN THE WOODS

Yvonne and Dewi left Aberystwyth station for Fairview Farm, the home and business of Gavin Hamer and his sons Thomas and Ieuan.

They arrived at the red-brick dwelling late morning, taking in its enormous size and the dilapidated state of the barns and outbuildings.

Gavin Hamer met them in the yard, sporting a thick jumper and flat cap against the weather. The skin on his cheeks was flaking and ruddy. The skin on the backs of his hands had aged more than was due for his fifty-three years.

"You're the police officers, then?" He greeted them, offering them his hand.

"We are." Yvonne smiled. "I'm DI Yvonne Giles and this is DS Dewi Hughes."

"Pleased to meet you. I'm Gavin. Gavin Hamer." He glanced back toward the farmhouse. "Do you want to go inside? It's cold out here, like." He pulled a face. "I'm okay, but then I'm used to it. Can't keep a lady out in this wind. It will rain any minute, too."

The DI nodded. "If you're sure it's all right, we'll go inside."

"Both my boys are out in it, on the tractors. They don't seem to notice."

"They're your children?" Yvonne asked as they entered the farmhouse kitchen. She took her coat off, giving it a shake.

"Aye, there's Thomas and Ieuan. They're not children any more. They're thirty-odd, now. They tell me to take it easy, but I only know farming. It's boring, not doing anything. I'd rather be busy. They tell me I get in the way." He laughed. The laugh turned into a cough that rattled his chest.

"Were you here in nineteen-ninety, Gavin?" The DI asked.

He took his cap off to reveal a full head of greying hair. "I was. I was helping Arthur, my father, in the eighties and nineties. My father ran the farm back then. He died of a heart attack twenty years ago, like."

"I'm sorry to hear that. What about your mum?"

"Mum passed away a few years back. She had diabetes."

"I'm sorry."

Gavin shrugged. "We get on with it, don't we?"

Yvonne nodded. "We do."

Dewi paused from writing. "Mr Hamer, can you tell us about the old Wood Cabin that used to stand near the bottom of Black Wood?"

"Oh, the old cabin? Yeah, what do you want to know?"

"Why was it demolished?"

Gavin rubbed the stubble on his chin. "Well, we kept having problems with it, didn't we?"

Yvonne frowned in concentration. "What sort of problems?"

"Someone kept killing animals in it. Dismembering them, like. They were taking the meat and leaving the hacked-up carcasses and blood everywhere inside the cabin."

"You said someone *kept* killing animals? How often did they do it?"

"About every six months, or so. After the third time, my dad had had enough. He got me to help him take it down. He wasn't in the best of health, so hadn't been using it much, anyway."

"What had he used it for?"

"Oh, he kept fishing stuff in it, fence-mending equipment, odd-and-sods, you know. It was a bit run down when the animal thieves came to steal the meat."

"What animals did they kill?"

"Sheep, I think it was. Hacked them to bits."

"So, there was sheep's blood all over the walls and floor?"

Gavin nodded. "It was awful, and the smell... I have never smelled anything quite that bad."

"Did you ever wonder whether someone had harmed a person in there?"

"A person?" He pulled a face. "No, the thought didn't occur to me."

"And police didn't test the blood?"

"Well, I don't suppose they felt the need to. I mean, it was pretty obvious what had happened. There were bits of hacked-up sheep everywhere."

"Did you or your father have any idea who might have done it?"

"I didn't, but my dad thought it might have been a devil-worshipping cult. You know, sacrificing animals and drinking the blood and all that."

"He didn't see anyone coming and going around there?"

Gavin shook his head. "No, I don't think so."

"What about you, did you see anyone hanging around?"

"No, never. I stayed down there a few times, too, in case anyone came by in the night. I had my father's shotgun with me. No-one came, though. That was before we knocked the old cabin down."

"It's a shame you had to do that." Yvonne pursed her lips.

"Oh, we built another one, further up the wood."

"Is it still there?"

"Yes, it is."

"Can we see it?"

"Sure. We keep it locked, so you'd have to take the key. It's here in the kitchen."

"Was the new cabin ever broken into?"

"Never. We worried for a time, in case it would be, but it never was. Whoever was doing it had either given up, or had gotten scared. The new cabin was closer to the house."

"I see."

"Do you want the key?"

"If we could please."

"No problem." He crossed the kitchen and grabbed a small set of keys from a hook next to the door. "There you go."

He gave them directions to the cabin. "Will you be needing me for anything else?"

"We will probably want to speak with you again. We'll be in touch. In the meantime, here is my card." She handed him one from her pocket. "Call me if you remember anything else you think is relevant."

"I will, for sure."

∾

As THEY WALKED AWAY from the farmhouse, in the direction they were pointed, Yvonne was deep in thought.

"Penny for them?" Dewi asked, picking his way around sheep poop.

"Well, Gavin Hamer said, they had slaughtered only three sheep there. I think it's safe to assume that the animals were being killed to cover up the murders of the young women. I suspect, in that case, only three of the five young women died there."

"You're right." Dewi frowned. So, where were the rest killed?

"Come one, let's catch Hamer before he disappears."

"You back again, already? I wasn't expecting you to bring the key back so quickly." Hamer grinned.

"Sorry, we haven't been to the cabin, yet. I wanted to ask you if you or anyone in your family had found blood anywhere else on your land, anywhere at all?"

He rubbed his forehead. "Well, em... My dad said they had killed some animals in the woods, I think. I'm sure it happened on more than one occasion, but I can't remember dates or anything. I think there was an oak tree where it had happened. There was blood on the tree, and it had soaked the ground. I went looking, and I didn't find the tree. We have lots of oaks in our woodland."

"And your dad didn't take you there?"

"No, I don't know to this day which tree my dad meant."

"Can I ask, is your current cabin similar to the one you took down?"

Hamer nodded. "It's almost identical. Dad liked things the way he liked them, everything just so. He put his fishing stuff and everything else in the new one, just as it had been in the old one."

"Thank you."

THEY LOCATED THE CABIN, as per their instructions from Gavin Hamer.

The padlock had ceased through lack of use. It took Dewi several attempts to get it to open. It gave way only because he whacked the padlock against the door with his fist, enabling the key to turn the rest of the way.

He bent over, nursing his hand.

"All in the line of duty." Yvonne grinned.

Dewi gave her a look.

What lay beyond the open door was a sizeable shed, some fifteen by twenty feet.

Popular with spiders, cobwebs littered everything, along with a significant layer of dust. The tools, however, were in a good, clean condition and hung on hooks fixed to the cabin sides, or lay atop the many shelves dotted about.

"Plenty of room to hold someone in a building like this." Yvonne shuddered. "No-one would hear their cries out here."

Dewi nodded. "The victim was probably gagged, too."

In her mind's eye, the DI could see the walls and floor spattered with blood. "It takes a special gall to kill someone, or have them killed, and then cover your tracks by slaughtering animals. I doubt, these days, they would have gotten away with it. They would test the blood for human material as a precaution."

"Probably." Dewi pursed his lips. "Thing is, if they find their shed broken into, and see bits of animal carcass everywhere, most people will take it as they find it. I don't blame the officers back then for not checking for human material, there were no human remains."

"True." Yvonne knelt to the floor, putting herself in the

position of a victim. "I wonder if the victims were aware of what was happening, or whether someone had hypnotised them so they wouldn't know their fate."

"Do you think it could have been a cult?" Dewi leaned his elbow on a shelf, his eyes wandering the cabin.

"I don't know. I hadn't considered it until now. Sheila Winters may have been indoctrinated into one. Perhaps, Pamela Mercer was, too."

"Have you heard anything else about her?"

Yvonne shook her head. "Susan Owen promised she would let me know if Mrs Mercer contacted her again. She used a hospital payphone to contact Susan. The payphone was in Bronglais Hospital, so we know she's in the area. I just hope she gets the courage to come forward. I'm desperate to know her story. If we have both Pamela and Sheila, we could fill the gaps and get some sort of timeline. I am convinced that someone was controlling those girls, I thought that person might be the deceased Hefin Thomas. Pamela has thrown a spanner into that works, however, and blown the scenario wide open again. I believe someone was making young girls kill each other, we just have to find out who that was."

THE DI WAS deep in thought on the journey back to Aberystwyth. Her mobile disturbed her thoughts as it rang and vibrated in her bag.

She fumbled for it, almost dropping the phone in her haste to put it to her ear. "Yvonne Giles."

"DI Giles? It's Susan Owen, the hypnotherapist-"

"Hi Susan, how can I help?" The DI held her breath.

"It's Pamela Mercer, she's been in touch. She has given

me her address and phone number, and asked that I give them to you, personally, and requested that we do not disclose her whereabouts to anyone else."

"I see, that's concerning. She sounds afraid of something. I won't pass the information on to anyone who isn't in my investigation team."

"I explained that her information would be safe with you. She was reluctant to tell me where she was, at first."

"Did she say why?"

"No, I'm afraid she didn't. I asked her if she was okay, and she said she was."

"Are you able to give me her number now?"

Susan was silent on the other end.

"Susan?"

"I can't... I promised her that I would only give it to you in person."

Yvonne sighed. "Very well, I understand. I will come to you."

HALF AN HOUR LATER, and Yvonne was ringing the bell at the porticoed entrance to Susan Owen's home.

Dewi waited for her in the car.

"Inspector Giles, come in." Susan led the DI along the hallway, her long hair held up in a tightly coiffed bun. "I've got the address in the library."

The sun's oblique rays burst through the individual panes of the large window, casting a window of light on the parquet floor. Yvonne watched as it reflected on a myriad dust particles swirling in the air.

"Careful," Susan smiled, "You're going into a trance."

"I am?" Yvonne tilted her head, raising an eyebrow.

"You were."

"Hmm." Yvonne pursed her lips, pondering that.

"Here you go." Susan handed her the page from her pad that contained Pamela Mercer's details. "Now remember, don't give them to anyone else, until you have spoken with Pamela yourself."

"Thank you." Yvonne pocketed the information.

"I should thank you," Susan said, holding open the library door for the DI.

"Oh?"

"Yes, after I spoke with you, last time, I attempted to catch up with colleagues I hadn't seen in months."

"You did?"

"Yes."

"And how did that go?" Yvonne asked as she traversed the hallway.

"It went well. We went for dinner at the Italian on North Parade, and have met for coffee, since. I've been so insular of late. I'd forgotten what it was like to have a social life."

"I'm pleased for you." Yvonne smiled, though something made her uneasy. She couldn't quite put her finger on what that was.

16

MISSING

Sarah Evans and Ifan Hughes greeted the DI as she returned to the station.

Ifan read from a sheet he was holding in front of him, his eyes shining. "Ma'am, we have identified three of the dead girls, based on their dental records."

"We have? That's great news. Who were they?"

"There were, Tracy Merrifield, Susan Lee, and Rachel Hardiman."

Yvonne, though glad of knowing their identities, felt a pang of regret when she thought of Tracy's elderly mother. This was the news Mrs Merrifield had been dreading. "I was aware of Tracy and Susan, and I've talked to people who knew them. Rachel Hardiman is a case I haven't chase up yet, but she was on the MisPer list, wasn't she? Can you remind me where she disappeared from?"

Sarah cleared her throat. "She vanished from a scrap-yard in Lampeter, in nineteen-ninety-one, ma'am."

"Really? The year after the first two disappeared?"

"That's right."

"Do you have the report of her disappearance to hand?"

"I do." Sarah passed her the file.

"Superb, thank you. I'll give this the once over, with a cuppa."

Ifan grinned. "I'll get the kettle on."

YVONNE SKIMMED the file until she came to John Hardiman's statement. His daughter Rachel had been helping him source spare parts for their truck from a local scrap merchants, just outside of a town called Lampeter, fifty minutes' drive and to the South of Aberystwyth.

Rachel's dad had left her alone for around fifteen minutes, while he entered the Portakabin to speak with the owner about parts he needed, and to make a cash payment.

In his statement, he said he had heard a car pull up outside, but had paid it no heed. Assuming it was another customer, he continued his chat with the owner.

When Hardiman returned to the yard to collect his daughter, she had vanished without a trace. He waited for an hour before telephoning the police, thinking she might have gotten bored, and gone for a walk.

He stated he did not see the vehicle which had entered the yard and had not taken notice of the engine, so could not guess at the make and model.

Yvonne sat back in her chair, her untouched cup of tea going cold.

"Any clues?" Dewi asked as he joined her.

She pushed her glasses atop her head. "Only that a car pulled into the yard while Rachel's father went inside to talk to the scrapyard owner. Rachel vanished while waiting for him to return. There's a good chance that vehicle took his daughter, but there is no proof of that it did, unfortunately."

"What did the dad think had happened?"

"Although he waited for police, in case his daughter had simply gone for a walk, he stated he thought it unlikely she would have wandered off. He said she would have been more likely to wander into the cabin to find him. When he left her, she was sitting on the bonnet of an old car, sunning herself."

"So, not looking like she was about to go hiking, then."

"Not at all."

"Do you think the car may have been the mustard Mini seen in Borth?"

Yvonne pursed her lips. "I don't know. It's something we should continue to check out. I haven't been able to link a Mini to any of the hypnotherapists on my radar."

"Could have belonged to a friend or relative?"

"Perhaps. Would you mind continuing to look into that for me? I'd be grateful."

Dewi nodded. "Of course not, leave it to me."

"Thanks, Dewi. In the meantime, I have an appointment with Pamela Mercer, who has been having flashbacks for some time, not unlike those Sheila Winters has been having. Perhaps, I ought to have someone else with me. Do you have time?"

"Sure, of course. I'll grab my coat."

As they left, Yvonne grabbed Ifan and Sarah. "Can you ask forensics to get onto the facial reconstruction labs? We need to know the identities of the two last sets of remains as soon as possible."

"Leave it to us." Sarah nodded. "We'll get on to them within the next ten minutes."

PAMELA MERCER'S lived in a small bay, two miles from

Aberystwyth. With its sand and shingle beaches, imposing cliffs, and many caravans, it was popular with tourists from all over the world. Mrs Mercer had chosen well.

The views took Yvonne's breath as they neared Pamela's clifftop home.

The DI checked her watch. They were ten minutes early. She hoped Mrs Mercer would be okay with that. The sea breeze would chill them to the bone if they waited outside.

As they approached the house from the front, the DI noticed the door was wide open. She wondered why, when the temperature was only five degrees centigrade at most.

When they got to a few feet away, they could hear the television blaring from somewhere inside the house and, though it was broad daylight, the lights were on.

The was bitterly cold. It gave her goose bumps.

Yvonne called out. "Mrs Mercer? Pamela? Hello?"

There was no reply.

"Hello?" she repeated.

Nothing.

"I'll search upstairs," Dewi said, his face grave.

"Okay, I'll continue down here." Yvonne nodded.

She moved from one room to the next, taking her time to check everywhere, in case something had happened to Mrs Mercer and she had collapsed.

Everything on the ground floor appeared orderly, with no sign of Pamela or that anything untoward had happened.

Having satisfied herself that the space was clear, the DI walked to the foot of the stairs. "Dewi?"

"Yes?" he called back.

"Anything up there?"

Her DS made his way down. "No. She made her bed, the rooms are tidy, but there is no sign of her."

"If her bed is made, I think it unlikely she slept in it. The fact the lights are on, suggest that she left in a hurry last night. The TV and wide-open door would support that. And, since it's highly unusual for anyone to pop out and leave their front door open and television blaring, I think we have to assume that something untoward has taken place. Though, goodness knows what that is. If she doesn't surface in the next twelve hours, we'll get SOCO in to go over the home. I have a bad feeling about this."

Dewi nodded. "I know what you mean."

"You didn't see any blood up there?"

"No, I didn't."

"Me neither." Yvonne scratched her head. "Let's look around outside, she may have popped out to do something and slipped or had a heart attack, or something."

"Right-oh."

They searched the grounds, and a shed at the back, which was unlocked, but there was no sign of Pamela Mercer. She had vanished.

When they had satisfied themselves that she was nowhere around, the DI donned gloves. Then, pulling the door until it was barely ajar, she telephoned dispatch, requesting officers guard the home until they could locate the owner.

"Think we'll need a search team?" Dewi asked when she finished, his eyes scanning the cliffs.

She pulled at her bottom lip. "Possibly, but I hope not. I will call Susan Owen to see if she has heard anything."

It took a minute for Susan to answer.

"It's Yvonne Giles, have you heard anything from Pamela Mercer since yesterday? Specifically, last night or very early this morning?"

"No, I haven't, why?" The higher pitch of Susan's voice betrayed her concern.

"She was not at home for the appointment with me. We found her front door wide open, the lights still on, and the TV blaring. I am concerned for her well-being."

"Were there signs of a struggle?" Susan asked, her breathing ragged.

"Not that we could detect, no. One scenario is that she answered the door to someone."

"Oh, no."

"Oh, no?"

"Well, I just mean that sounds ominous."

"Did she show signs of dementia when she communicated with you recently?"

"Not that I could tell. She seemed to have all her faculties. I didn't spend a long time with her, but I didn't notice any mental absences when she was talking to me."

"Did you mention to anyone else that she had been in touch with you?"

"I might have mentioned it to a few colleagues, in connection with the flashbacks she was having. I went for lunch with several therapists the other day, and we discussed the strangeness of her case."

"I'll need the names of all those who were at the meal, if that is okay."

"Yes, but why? Surely, you don't think her disappearance has something to do with a hypnotherapist, do you?"

Yvonne didn't wish to say too much. "One of them might have spoken to her, since the meal. I think it more likely she has wandered off, perhaps during one of her flashbacks." It was weak. The DI knew it. She hoped Susan didn't notice.

Susan told her the names of the therapists who were there.

They were practitioners the DI had spoken to in the last few weeks. "All right. Thank you, Susan. Listen, if Pamela contacts you again, could you please telephone me right away?"

"I will, of course."

As Yvonne ended the call, she made mental plans to interview the therapists again. First, however, she needed to organise the search for Mrs Mercer.

17

RECONSTRUCTIONS

B ack in the Aberystwyth incident room, Callum and
Dai travelled from Newtown to join the team.
Yvonne tasked them with chasing down
medical information for the three identified victims, Tracy
Merrifield, Susan Lee, and Rachel Hardiman and, specifically, whether any of them were receiving treatment via
hypnotherapy in the months prior to their murders.

Callum made notes. "What about the two women we
haven't identified? Any news on when we will have details so
we can chase those up?"

Yvonne nodded. "We've asked a reconstruction team in
Glasgow to help. They are working on the digital faces as we
speak. Because of the speed at which they can work, we
hope to have good likenesses for the girls within the next
twenty-four to forty-eight hours."

"That quickly?"

The DI nodded. "It takes about four days from the time
they scan the remains, apparently. They said they might get
it done in three. They have had the images two days
already."

Callum raised his eyebrows. "I'm impressed."

"Me too. As soon as the public has identified them from the reconstructions, we can chase up their medical information, including whether they have been subject to hypnosis."

"You've got a working theory, I can tell..." Callum tilted his head. "What are you thinking?"

"I have a hunch that someone was taking advantage of girls they knew to be hypnotisable."

"Their therapist?"

"Perhaps, or someone who knew they were undergoing treatment, and had a working knowledge of hypnosis techniques."

"Interesting." Callum turned to go.

"Oh, and... thanks for your help." Yvonne gave him a smile. "It is good to have the whole team on this."

Callum grinned. "Happy to be here, ma'am."

PAMELA MERCER HAD NOT RETURNED HOME by late afternoon.

Yvonne requested a uniformed search team to scour the bottom of the cliffs, below Mrs Mercer's house, along with the land surrounding it. The DI was even more concerned, since they had found Pamela's handbag in a hallway cupboard with her phone and house keys. It wasn't looking good.

Dewi donned gloves and flicked through the numbers of her most recent calls and texts.

If Mrs Mercer didn't show up, the phone would go to the lab for further analysis.

"Anything significant?"

Dewi shook his head. "Not as far as texts are concerned.

She had no meetings, or appointments set up via text. She phoned a mobile two days ago and a different mobile telephoned *her* the day before that. I'll get the lab to source those numbers for us."

"Okay, good." Yvonne ran her hands through her hair. "Where is she?"

THEIR CONCERNS ESCALATED WHEN, after eighteen hours of searching, Pamela Mercer was still missing and had not made contact.

Sarah and Ifan searched for relatives, in case she had gone to them. They knew Mrs Mercer to be reclusive, shunning face-to-face contact, mostly. This made their job much more difficult. The relatives they had spoken to stated that they hadn't heard from Pam for years.

It was therefore vital they find out who she had spoken to on her mobile in the days before her disappearance.

IN HER ARMS, Yvonne carried the files of the last of the women named by their families following facial reconstruction.

The sobering details were all too familiar.

Nineteen-year-old Tonya Leek came from Llandinam, a small village located five miles south of Newtown.

Tonya, who was to be married that summer, had vanished on her way to the village store, where she planned to buy a birthday card for her brother.

In full health, and with no medical issues, there had

been no obvious reason for her disappearance. Her family stated they believed someone had abducted her.

Her fiancé, Alan Jones, worked for the local coal merchants. In his statement, he said that had waved to her from the yard as she walked along the pavement adjoining the main highway. She appeared happy and smiling and waved back to him.

Alan said that was the last time he saw her.

Callum and Dai confirmed that she was not and never had been subject to hypnotherapy.

Neither had Gabriel Layton, a twenty-year-old hairdresser from Caersws, a village on the road to Aberystwyth and, like Llandinam, approximately five miles from Newtown.

Gabriel had disappeared after leaving Cutz Hairdresser's in Caersws at six o'clock in the evening, after finishing her shift. Her walk home would have involved part of the main road to Carno. She never arrived.

Yvonne sat back in her chair, pushing her glasses atop her head. She had to revise her thinking regarding what might have happened to the women. It would seem that the murder victims had not been subject to hypnotherapy, unlike their self-confessed killers.

What she did not know was whether there were more women out there who *had* been under hypnotherapy and killed other girls.

As for Rachel Hardiman, Tracy Merrifield, and Susan Lee, Callum and Dai could find no links to hypnotism and, as far as anyone knew, they had no medical concerns and had never been subject to hypnotherapy.

Yvonne pondered whether the someone had simply pulled the girls into a car, or otherwise persuaded them to get into a vehicle. If so, who had done the persuading, and how did the abductor bring them under control. Perhaps more than one person acted together to carry out abductions.

She put this idea to the others in the morning briefing, tasking her DCs with going through all the witness statements, looking for any that mentioned vehicles, and their occupants, seen in the area during the period in which the girls vanished.

18

PSYCHOLOGY

uring the briefing, Ifan Hughes let them know
that several mustard-coloured Minis had been
registered to a car rental firm in Aberystwyth.

"Good work, Ifan." Yvonne scratched her head. "Do we know who rented them? Does the firm still exist?"

The DC checked his notes. "It does. The firm is Auto Rentals, and they would normally have been able to tell us who hired them as they keep all of their records. However, the firm suffered a dramatic fire, which destroyed all paperwork up to nineteen ninety-six. They lost everything. As a result, we can't chase down who hired those vehicles."

The DI frowned. "Did they know how the fire started?"

"Whoever started the fire, did so with accelerants, but they never found the culprit or culprits. Insurance inspectors investigated the owner. They cleared him of wrongdoing. They never solved the arson."

"I see. Okay, thanks. I wonder if the rumours of the mustard Mini seen in Borth spooked someone. There was a Crimewatch programme about the disappearances in ninety-six, wasn't there?"

Ifan nodded. "The previous investigating officer mentioned it in the file."

"Could you go through the information that came through on the hotlines, specifically in relation to the tan Mini?"

"Will do, ma'am."

FOLLOWING THE MORNING BRIEFING, Yvonne received a phone call.

"Yvonne Giles?"

"Hello, it's Susan Owen."

"Susan? How can I help?"

"I understand that Pamela Mercer is now officially a missing person, am I right?"

"Yes, that's right. She still hasn't shown up. We have teams out looking for her."

"Yes, well, I thought you should know that it's not the first time she has run off."

Yvonne frowned. "What do you mean?"

Susan stuttered. "W-Well, she has disappeared before. Last time she went, she was under treatment with me in nineteen-ninety."

"Really?"

"Yes, she didn't return for several weeks."

"Where did she go?"

"I don't know. She never told me."

"Why did you leave it until now to inform me of this?"

"I'd forgotten, it was a long time ago."

The DI's brown remained furrowed in concentration. "Do you have notes from her sessions, back then?"

There was a several-second silence on the other end.

"Susan?"

"I don't think I have records going back that far. I think my husband did a clear-out years ago. He shredded any files that were that old."

"No computer records?"

"Not that far back, no. I began digitising notes, but not until ninety-eight. It wasn't as far back as nineteen-ninety."

"When she left, last time, did she take her personal effects? Money? Bag?"

"I don't know. I only know that she abandoned the house without locking it and left the lights on."

"Was she in a trance?"

"What?"

"Was she hypnotised? It seems odd that she would go without making her house safe."

"I didn't hypnotise her, if that is what you are thinking."

"I wonder if the time she first disappeared coincided with when she believes she killed someone?"

Susan cleared her throat. "Well, I wouldn't know about that."

"Did she behave abnormally, after she returned in nine-teen-ninety? Can you remember that far back?"

"I remember her having absences."

"What, disappearing again?"

"No, I meant mental absences. When I was talking to her, she would zone out. She was doing this a lot. More than before, and it was not an intended trance."

"What did you do?"

"I would call her back. She was having what the French call Petit mal."

"I see. And did she explain her disappearance to you?"

"No, she didn't, I'm afraid."

"Did you ask her while she was in trance?"

"No."

"Why not?"

"I was carrying out specific work from a script I had pre-prepared. Pamela had not given me permission to deviate from that script or to extract information which she was not ready to disclose."

"And yet, her disappearance may have been anxiety-related. Isn't that right?"

"Of course, but whatever her reasons for going, I was treating her anxiety. If her disappearance related to her condition, she would have been less likely to go again, in any event. I was engaged in helping her, not squeezing her for information. I'm not a police officer, Inspector."

As Yvonne put away her phone, she pondered the fact that Susan Owen had held back such an important detail when she knew that Pamela Mercer had gone missing again. If Susan had been a man, she might have just topped the therapist suspect list.

Sheila Winters set down her bag and coat on the floor between herself and the duty solicitor.

Yvonne gave her a reassuring smile as she readied her note papers and switched on the digital recorder, introducing everyone.

"Thank you for coming in for this informal interview, Sheila. You say you have regained more memories?"

"Yes." Sheila leaned forward, resting her elbows on the interview room table, cupping her chin with her hands.

"Do you want to tell me about them?"

"I remember more about the room where I was having hypnotherapy."

"Okay..."

"It was large, around fifty square feet."

"Go on."

"There were two treatment beds. Couches, if you will, and windows on two sides of the room. There may have been a bay window to the front, which faced a road. I know it faced a road, but we were not on the ground floor. I think we may have been two floors up. I could hear occasional traffic and see the top of a tree."

"Do you remember any other scenery from the street outside?"

Sheila shook her head. "No, only the tree. I think it was about ten years old, judging by the width of the trunk, and it was tall. I could see the canopy, from where I was, while lying on the couch. I say canopy, but I think the branches were bare in a lot of my memories. The room was dark, save for the light coming from a small side lamp and the street-lights outside. Car lights sometimes travelled the length of the ceiling and down the walls."

"You said for many of the memories. Does that mean that for some of them the canopy was full?"

"Yes, the leaves were on the tree and the room was in daylight. It felt like evening or maybe early morning."

"Can you orient these memories in time? Have you any idea how distant these memories were from the ones involving violence?"

"I can't be sure, but I think the winter memories came first, then the summer sessions. I know the murder took place in summer. I remember how the forest was teeming with life."

"When you think back to who you were before therapy, what time of year was it? I am talking about when you were considering seeking help to stop smoking?"

"I believe it was summer."

"Okay. Were you told how long you would have to wait for treatment?"

"Yes, I was told six months."

The DI nodded. "That would fit with your treatment beginning in winter, and with your mental timeline."

"Yes."

"What about your therapist? Can you see him in the memory of the daylight session? Can you describe him?"

"He's sitting in the corner, he has windows either side of him."

"Can you see his face?"

Sheila shook her head. "He appears dark, like a silhouette. I can't understand this, because the room is so filled with light."

"What about his clothes? What is he wearing?"

Sheila shrugged. "I don't know."

"But the room is filled with light, you said. Can you try again, now? Try to see him in the image."

Sheila frowned in concentration.

Finally, she shook her head. "It's no use, I just can't see any details. It's like... It's like..."

"Like what?" Yvonne prompted, her voice low.

"It's like he's blocked me from seeing him."

"You mean you think he used hypnotic suggestion to hide himself from you?"

"Yes."

"Can you remember him saying anything along those lines?"

"No, no, I can't."

"Okay, what about the room? Is there any other furniture, besides the two couches?"

"There are books piled on a table, along with papers and a printer. I hear a printer whirring in the background of some memories. I can see it in the day-lit room, too. It is to the right of the therapist as I'm looking at him."

"Do you have any memories from before any of the sessions? Can you remember thinking to yourself that you needed to get ready to see someone for therapy? It might give you a name."

"No, nothing about getting ready."

"Do you have any other memories from that year?"

"Yes, but none that I can tie in to therapy."

"I see."

"I think my memory was being altered after each session, to make me forget it."

The DI nodded. "Perhaps."

"I'm sorry, I'm not being much help, am I?"

Yvonne smiled to reassure her. "On the contrary, every piece of information you give me is helping to build a picture. Tell me, does the name Pamela Mercer mean anything to you?"

Sheila screwed her face up, her eyes moving to the ceiling. "Hmm, no, it doesn't ring any bells at all."

"What about Pam, or Pammy?"

"Nothing, I'm afraid." Sheila shrugged. "I think I have given you all I can, for now."

Yvonne nodded. "Very well, we'll leave it there for today. Thank you, for coming in."

～

TASHA PUT her arm around Yvonne's shoulders as they sat

on the couch together watching the evening news. "You look tired and preoccupied. Want to talk about it?"

Yvonne sighed, leaning her head on the psychologist's shoulder. "One of my potential witnesses to murder has disappeared. I didn't get the chance to speak to her. She spoke to the woman who used to be her hypnotherapist, saying she'd been having flashbacks of killing someone, following the media coverage on the remains we found in Black Wood. After that, she disappeared. We had a search ongoing for her, but the DCI has scaled it back, since her former therapist stated that my witness had done this before. I am still concerned for her welfare, however."

"I see. Who was her therapist?"

"A lady called Susan Owen. She no longer sees her for hypnotherapy, but she was seeing her at the time during which the girls in the wood were murdered, and when Pamela said she thinks she hurt someone."

"Okay. Why did Pamela tell her former therapist this? Why didn't she go straight to the police?"

The DI pursed her lips. "Good question, I don't know. I'm also concerned that Susan Owen felt it unnecessary to tell me about the first occasion Pamela rain off, even though I specifically asked her about Pamela, on the day she disappeared. Susan didn't tell me about the previous disappearance until earlier today, three days after Pam went missing."

"Did she tell you why she left it so late?"

"She said she had forgotten the earlier incident until this morning."

"Really?"

"Yes, and somehow, I find that hard to believe. I mean, wouldn't a previous disappearance be your first thought? It's highly significant when they have done that before, surely?"

"You'd have thought so, but I guess it is possible that Susan forgot. We are talking thirty years, after all."

"Hmm."

"It's also possible..." Tasha closed her mouth.

"What?" Yvonne prompted.

"Well, I don't know whether it's..."

"What?" Yvonne grabbed Tasha's ribs. "I swear, I'll tickle you if you don't spit it out."

"Okay, okay." Tasha laughed, but her face straightened immediately. "You know, it is just possible that Susan Owen could be your mystery therapist."

"What do you mean?"

"Well, what if she were the one who worked with Pam and Sheila?"

"She worked with Pam, but Sheila was Hefin Thomas's case."

"Yes, but you told me a few days ago that you were considering the possibility that someone influenced both girls, knowing they were susceptible to hypnosis."

"Right, except that the person I am looking for was a male, according to Sheila Winters."

"I know, but is it not possible for a hypnotist to change their subject's perception such that the therapist could, if they wanted, appear to be a male instead of female? They could have the subject convinced of many things that were not the case."

"Can they do that?"

"Sure, they can give them an alternative image of themselves, even changing their hair colour or style. Why not gender? The subject will see what the hypnotist is suggesting to the subconscious."

"So, Susan Owen could have made Sheila believe she was being hypnotised by a man.

"I believe so. If I were you, I would ask another hypnosis expert, one who isn't on your suspect list. Don't take my word for it in case I am wrong."

Yvonne rubbed her cheek. "Wow, Tasha, you've really got me thinking. If the subject's perception can be altered to that degree, then why not also the time of day, time of year, and even the location of the sessions?"

"Theoretically, they could change those things in the subject's mind, though they may not have done. We should be careful of adding unnecessary complications, but it is worth bearing in mind as you gather more evidence. I think you have to give weight to what the subjects tell you, but remember some details may have been open to manipulation by the therapist. Keep all options open."

"I will, thank you. By the way, I meant to tell you when I came home that the DCI has said you can join the investigation. I think the pressure from the media has been getting to him. He'll say yes to virtually anything that speeds up the investigation."

"Oh, thanks..."

Yvonne put her hands to her cheeks. "I didn't mean it like that, I-"

Tasha laughed. "It's okay, I'm pulling your leg. I cannot wait to help. This sounds like one of the most fascinating and baffling cases we have worked on."

Yvonne nodded. "You can say that again."

"This sounds like one of the most-"

"Hilarious." Yvonne pulled a face. "Come here, I've got some serious tickling to do."

19

LOSING WITNESSES

Dewi found Yvonne as she waded through old witness statements from the families of the dead girls. "Ma'am, We've heard from the CPS. They say we don't have enough to charge Sheila Winters with murder."

The DI nodded. "I'm inclined to agree with them. I don't believe she was culpable, but we are having a hard time proving anything at the moment, even that she committed a murder. It will be tough to prove that someone else was controlling her as I believe may be the case. Has anything come back from forensics?"

Dewi ran his hands through his hair. "They have foreign fibres from some of the clothing items, but no usable DNA. The problem is, the clothing worn by the perp was likely discarded years ago. I mean, nobody wears the same shirt for thirty years, right?"

"What about carpet fibres? Any of those? We use carpets for a longer period. We could get lucky."

"I can't remember off the top of my head. I think they found six distinct fibres. They are still working to identify the materials they may have come from. I'll get the interim report and put it on your desk."

"Thank you. I appreciate it. I'll give Sheila a call, let her know that she won't need to attend court."

"Right-oh. I'll make you a brew."

YVONNE TRIED several times to telephone Mrs Winters on both her landline and her mobile. Sheila wasn't answering.

Her sergeant came back with the teas and set one down for her.

"She's not answering, Dewi."

"Maybe she's busy." He winced at his hot tea.

"Yes, maybe." The DI thought about Pamela Mercer. She couldn't help worrying about Sheila. "I think I might pop to see her. Check that she is all right."

Dewi nodded. "If we can just drink our tea first, I'll come with you. The sun's shining, it'll be good to get out and have a change from wading through files."

"Right, drink up."

THE DRIVE to Waun Fawr took them ten minutes.

Sheila occupied a semi-detached house on a tiny estate. They parked the car as close as they could and approached the front door. It was ten-fifteen in the morning.

"The curtains are closed." Dewi hesitated at the front door. "Do we knock, or not?"

Yvonne pursed her lips. "Yes, she might sleep late."

"Shall I pop round the back? It's usually where the

kitchen is. She might be having breakfast and just not gotten around to opening her curtains, yet."

The DI nodded. "Good idea. Let's take a peek."

They walked the small pathway at the side of the house to the back garden, bounded by a high wooden fence.

"Mrs Winters?" Dewi called, letting her know they were there, so they wouldn't startle her. "Mrs Winters? It's the police."

The kitchen blinds were open.

Dewi traversed the lawn to peer in. "The light is on in there," he said. "I can't see Sheila, though."

Yvonne knocked the back door. "Mrs Winters? Sheila? It's Yvonne Giles. Are you there?"

On receiving no answer, the DI tried the door handle. To her surprise, the door opened.

"Mrs Winters? It's Yvonne Giles."

Still no answer, but in the background, Yvonne could hear what she thought was a radio.

She moved through the hallway to the room the sound was coming from. "Sheila?"

It wasn't a radio; it was the television. There was no sign of Sheila Winters.

The DI ran back to the hallway, calling up the stairs. "Mrs Winters? Sheila?"

She flew up the stairs, two at a time, entering each room and finding them empty. Sheila wasn't anywhere in the house.

Yvonne called down the stairs. "Is she there, Dewi?"

"Nowhere down here, ma'am"

There was no sign of a disturbance. The bed had not been slept in.

"She could have popped out," Dewi offered.

Yvonne nodded. "It's possible, but I'm worried for her." She perched on the edge of the couch.

"Shall we wait to see if she comes back?"

"Let's give her fifteen minutes. If she's popped out to the local shop, she should be back about then. I wouldn't think she would leave the television and lights on if she intended being out for longer."

They waited for twenty-five minutes and Sheila had still not returned. They couldn't see her handbag anywhere.

Yvonne tried phoning her again, to no avail. "I know exactly what the DCI will think." She stood up, clicking her phone off.

"That she skipped bail?"

She nodded. "Her court date was tomorrow."

"She is probably scared of going to court. Many people are, even when they are not appearing for murder."

The DI shook her head. "Makes no sense. She came to me because she felt horrified at what she remembered. I don't believe she would skip bail now. I am worried that someone might want her out of the way, and that someone must know she is having flashbacks."

"Susan Owen?"

"Perhaps, she's climbed higher on my suspect list recently, but it could equally have been one of her colleagues. She said she talked to other therapists at a dinner last week."

"Loose tongues..."

"Exactly."

"I'll call it in." Dewi pulled out his phone. "We'll get local uniform to keep an eye out for her. With any luck, she'll turn up."

Yvonne nodded. "But if not, both our witnesses-come-killers are missing."

"Oh, I wasn't expecting to see you again so soon." Susan Owen stared at the DI, wide-eyed.

"Can I come in?"

"Er... Yes, of course." Susan stepped back to allow the DI into the hallway of her home. "What can I do for you?"

Yvonne's eyes were already scanning all around. "Sheila Winters has gone missing and it's her Court date. Have you seen her?"

Susan looked at her, open-mouthed. "No, I haven't seen her."

"Are you sure?"

"Yes, I am sure, Inspector. What's all this about? You don't think I made her disappear, surely?"

"I am asking everyone who might have seen her. What concerns me, is that her television and lights were still on. Uncannily similar to Pamela Mercer's disappearance, don't you think?"

Susan frowned. "Wow, that is odd. But, if you are wondering if I made them walk out of their homes, don't you think I would have had them turn off their TV sets? And their lights?"

Yvonne tilted her head. "Is that the sort of thing they might do if they were in trance when they left?"

"What, leave their lights on?"

"Yes."

Susan rubbed her chin. "Well, it is possible. Are you thinking someone put them in a trance? Or do you think they might have hypnotised themselves?"

"Can they do that?"

"What?"

"Hypnotise themselves?"

"Yes, in theory, anyone can hypnotise themselves. In fact, even in a session with a trained hypnotist, it is the client who puts themselves in the trance. Obviously, that is with the guidance of the therapist, but they do it themselves. You are responsible for your trance, not your therapist."

"What would have made them self-hypnotise?"

Susan shrugged. "I don't know." She pulled at her lower lip. "Someone could have hypnotised them on an occasion before they disappeared and given specific instructions to leave the house on a certain time and day."

"Really?"

"Yes, it's perfectly possible. The subconscious is very good at keeping time. However, they would also have been told where to go. Otherwise, why give them instructions at all?"

"Do you think they may have gone to the same place?"

Sheila stepped back. "I don't know, I'm just suggesting possibilities. You've put me on the spot, Inspector."

"And you are sure you haven't seen them at all?"

Susan shook her head.

"They're not here?"

"No." The muscles tightened in Susan's face. "I have work to do, Inspector."

"Then, I'll leave you to get on with it." The DI's eyes pierced Susan Owen. "If you hear from either of them, be sure and let me know, immediately."

20

ALL ARE SUSPECT

Yvonne wanted to speak to the hypnotherapists again. She took both Dewi and Tasha with her. She especially wanted Tasha's opinion of them and her assessment of their behaviour, desperate as she was for any sort of clue.

As they arrived on the industrial estate, Yvonne reminded herself of the things she wanted to ask George Langley and his business partner, Brian Watson. She wanted them in the room together, so she could witness the dynamic between them. This way, she hoped to tell if they were colluding to cover something up.

The receptionist showed them to the meeting room, telling them that George and Brian would be with them shortly.

Yvonne checked her watch.

"Sorry to keep you waiting." Brian burst in. "George is just finishing with a client, he'll be with us in a few minutes." He held his hand out to each of them.

The DI noted the sheen on Brian's head, musing that it must have been warm in his treatment room.

When George finally joined them, he seated himself without ceremony, staring at Yvonne in expectation.

The DI introduced Tasha and Dewi, though she did not explain that Tasha was a psychologist. "Thank you, for taking the time out of your busy schedules." She smiled at the two hypnotists. "First, I'd to ask you if you've seen either of these two women in recent days?" She pushed photographs of Pamela Mercer and Sheila Winters towards them.

George and Brian studied the photos, frowning in concentration, and flicking glances at each other.

George shrugged. "No, I'm afraid not. Who are they?"

Yvonne looked at Brian.

He gave her a blank stare before raising his eyebrows.

The DI rubbed her cheek. "They are Sheila Winters and Pamela Mercer. Both women have vanished in odd circumstances."

George gasped. "Why have you come to us? Did you think we knew these women?"

Yvonne nodded. "I thought you might recognise them. They have been subject to hypnotherapy in the past and, though not your clients, I wondered if they might have been here to ask for treatment?"

Langley looked at Watson. "Have you seen them, Brian?"

Brian shook his head, but picked up both the photographs, pushing his glasses further up his nose to peer at them again. "They haven't been in here."

"Have either of them telephoned you? Do you recognise the names?"

They shook their heads in perfect time, like synchronised swimmers.

"Have either of you ever owned a Mini?"

"No." George was emphatic. "Never."

"My wife had one." Brian nodded. "I got to drive it occasionally, but I always preferred a bigger motor."

The DI turned her full attention on Brian. "I bet you don't remember the colour of your wife's Mini?"

Brian screwed his face up, looking at the ceiling. "I believe it was blue."

"Are you sure?"

"Yes, it was blue. Why do you ask?"

Yvonne turned the page in her notebook. "Have either of you ever been to Black Wood?"

"Black wood?" George frowned. "Why Black Wood? Wait a minute, isn't that where you found remains recently? That was where five girls were murdered, right?"

The DI nodded. "It was."

George leaned back in his chair. "Do you think one of us had something to do with those deaths? Is that where you are going with this?"

Yvonne held up a hand. "I'm simply asking the question. I'll be straight with you." She pointed to the photographs. "The two women in these photographs disappeared form their homes, a couple of days apart. They left their homes unlocked, the lights on and, in one case, with a television set blaring away. This is highly unusual, I am sure you will agree. It might be silly, but we are wondering if they might have been in a hypnotic trance when they let their homes."

Brian laughed. "Why would they have been in a trance? Do you think someone hypnotised them to up and leave? Or, perhaps, you think they hypnotised themselves?"

"We don't know. That's why we are approaching the experts on the subject."

"Sorry." George folded his arms. "I do not know who these women are, or why they left their homes."

Brian shook his head. "Me, neither. I certainly haven't

been to their homes and, to my knowledge, I have never seen either of them for any reason whatsoever."

George nodded. "Same here. I honestly can't help you. If I could help you, I promise you, I would."

Yvonne could see she was getting nowhere and rose to leave. "I'm afraid we don't have a lot of time and we need to get off. But, if you think of anything that might be helpful, could you contact us immediately?"

George rose to see them out. "Yes, of course we could, Inspector."

"WHAT DID YOU THINK?" Yvonne asked Tasha and Dewi as they walked back to their car.

Tasha tilted her head. "I think they are likely to have their secrets, but I think they were genuine in their assertions that they don't know where Sheila and Pamela are."

Dewi nodded. "They seemed clueless."

Yvonne paused and pulled out her mobile. She phoned Callum.

"Ma'am?"

"Callum, could you and Dai put a trace on the four mobile phone numbers on the post-it on my desk? The names and numbers are there. Monitor which phone towers they ping and leave the details for me for when I get back."

"Will do, ma'am. Do you want us to call you about any place specific?"

"Only if you think it urgent, we are still talking to some of them."

"Okay, no problem."

IN CONTRAST with Susan Owen's porticoed, Georgian home, Simon Hopkins' place was an ultra-modern box, all glass, steel and reinforced concrete.

On one wall of his airy lounge hung a large screen.

"I use it for online hypnosis sessions." Simon informed them. "It makes it feel like the clients are in the room with me. It works really well."

Yvonne's eyes travelled the sparsely furnished room. "Did you say all of your clients are online, now? Mister Hopkins?"

"Simon, please. Yes, Inspector, practically all of them. Occasionally I see people in a treatment room here, but these days that is a rare occurrence. Would you like coffee?"

"No, thank you." Yvonne perched herself on the corner suite.

Tasha also declined a hot drink.

Dewi accepted.

When Simon returned with Dewi's coffee, he pulled up a chair, so he was opposite the three of them. "This feels very formal, I feel like I'm being interviewed for a job. How can I help you?"

Yvonne glanced up at the screen. "Does the name Pamela Mercer mean anything to you?"

Simon undid the cuffs on his shirt sleeves and rolled them up. "Pamela Mercer? No, I'm afraid it doesn't. Should it? I mean, I get through a lot of clients now that I work online. I may forget the odd name over the course of a few years."

The DI continued. "Do you remember I asked you recently about a lady called Sheila Winters?"

"Yes, I do. The woman who lost a portion of her memory."

"That's right. She's missing. Gone AWOL."

"Oh, really?" He grimaced. "Is that a memory thing again?"

Yvonne shrugged. "We're not sure. All we know is she abandoned her home and didn't take any of her bag or her purse."

He frowned. "Oh, dear."

"Exactly. The thing is, we are very concerned about her. What we know is she was trying to regain lost memories, and we wondered whether she had approached hypnotherapists for help to regain those memories."

He shook his head. "She hasn't been to see me, I'm afraid."

"And she hasn't spoken to you on the phone or via video call?"

"No, she hasn't."

"I see. And you are sure that you haven't communicated with anyone called Pamela Mercer in recent days?"

"I'm sure. Unless, she used a different name?"

Yvonne pulled out the photographs of Sheila and Pamela. "That's Pam, there." She pointed to the second photo. "This is Sheila Winters."

He inspected them for several minutes, examining first one photo, then the other. "No, I'm afraid I don't recognise either of these women."

He handed the pictures back to Yvonne, who pocketed them.

"How many sessions do you do in a day?" she asked, once more looking at the screen.

"Oh, between four and eight, usually. I've got one scheduled in the next ten minutes," he said, looking at his watch.

"Well, in that case, we won't keep you."

They rose to leave.

"Sorry I couldn't be more help." He smiled, but it didn't quite reach his eyes.

21

TRANCE

*S*usan grabbed her bag and keys, turning to take a last look around her hallway before closing the front door and locking it.

She checked her phone, breathing a sigh of relief at the blank screen. No demands.

Heart thumping, she strode to her car, unlocking it well before she got there. Time was running out.

She put her foot down as much as she dared, without drawing attention to herself. The eyes of the police were the last thing she needed.

As the sun went down, she left the bustle of Aberystwyth behind, taking the road for Borth. She would get there in the light, but had a large torch in her glove compartment, ready for the evening gloom.

As soon as she hit the country roads, she could floor the accelerator. Timing was everything.

Susan barely noticed the road or the scenery, her brain on automatic.

She finally reached the lay-by, parked, and jumped out. Glad of her walking boots and thick waterproof trousers, she set off up the muddy track, heading with a feeling of dread towards the damp forest.

Walking the up the lane, her ears pricked at every swish and flutter. Several times she disturbed birds and jumped when they squawked away.

As darkness fell, she switched on the torch.

YVONNE FINISHED her paperwork as Tasha joined her ready for the journey home. Dewi came to say goodnight before he, too, would leave.

Callum came dashing in. "Ma'am, Susan Owen's phone has pinged the tower near Black Wood."

"What?" Yvonne frowned. "Black Wood? What on earth is she doing up there? It's an odd time of night to be going for a walk in the middle of nowhere."

Tasha nodded. "And it's getting dark."

The DI flicked her gaze between Tasha and Dewi. "Pamela and Sheila?"

Tasha pursed her lips. "You don't think the women are there, do you?"

Yvonne rubbed her chin. "I don't know... Then again, why not? They are the two people who could, if we are correct, incriminate a killer-by-proxy. Wouldn't it make sense to hypnotise them into going somewhere they could dispose of them?"

"But, Susan Owen? Really?" Dewi was having a hard time seeing their criminal therapist as a woman.

Yvonne pushed her glasses atop her head. "It's not the first time we've had reason to question her behaviour." The DI grabbed her coat. "Callum, get onto the DCI, we need an ARV and a dog team to Black Wood, as soon as possible."

"There may be a problem there." Callum grimaced. "The nearest ARV is attending an armed domestic in Machynlleth."

"Okay, well, get onto the DCI, anyway. He can organise another ARV to attend as soon as possible. In the meantime, I'll go there myself. Ask for a uniform team to back me up, will you? But ask for them to hang back until I instruct them further. The last thing we want is for those women to come to harm, if they are there. We don't know what they may be facing."

"I'm coming with you." Dewi put on his mac.

"Yes, me too." Tasha grinned. "The 'A' Team."

Yvonne nodded. "Thank you both, I appreciate it."

"Okay, let's go."

PAMELA AND SHEILA *approached to within fifteen feet of each other.*

The former held a heavy axe with a long handle. The latter, a hunting knife.

In the background, a dark shape took a few paces, gaining a better view.

"You can begin." The voice was calm. Soothing.

The two women interrupted the night's silence with grunts and heavy breathing as they circled each other, wildly swinging their weapons, trying to gain an advantage. Their eyes were wide, and their lower lips, limp.

Pamela's knife chafed Sheila's upper arm. She barely noticed as she swung the axe at Pamela midriff. It missed.

"Go deeper." A voice called out. A different voice. Not the shape's voice.

Pamela and Sheila paused, their weapon arms dropping limp to their sides.

The shape drew back.

"Drop your weapon, Pamela. Drop your weapon, Sheila." The new voice instructed.

Both women allowed their blades to fall to the floor.

The dark shape moved from tree to tree, remaining in the shadows, away from the torchlight.

Susan Owen approached the women, her heart thumping between her breasts. She kicked away first the knife and then the axe. The axe was too heavy to go very far. She had to kick it again.

A gloved hand covered her mouth and gripped with vice-like ferocity.

Susan gasped, biting at the fingers. They let her go, but it proved a temporary reprieve.

Someone grabbed her hair from behind as a punch landed on her back. She dropped to her knees, pain searing her lower body.

"Perhaps, they should kill you first." His voice was low and deceptively soft as he said this in her ear.

He pulled hard on her hair and Susan felt like she might lose her scalp.

She squealed in pain.

"It's rude to interrupt another therapist's session."

"I know you," she said, trying to catch her breath. "You're Hopkins. The police are on their way."

"Are they? Funny, I don't see any. And my name is Simon. It's rude to refer to me by my surname. No-one has done that to me since boarding school." He threw her to the ground, kicking her in the ribs to ensure she stayed there.

He grabbed the hunting knife. "You shouldn't have come, Susan. This isn't your business."

She held her rib. It felt like he had broken it. Talking and breathing hurt. "It's people like you who bring our profession into disrepute. We don't harm people, we help them." Susan threw up over her thighs.

The shape turned his attention to Pamela and Sheila. "Sheila, get the axe."

Sheila obeyed.

Pamela stayed where she was. Still as the trees.

Hopkins pointed his gloved hand towards Susan Owen. "Sheila, strike her."

"Stop," Susan ordered. "Sheila, I want you to drop the axe."

A look of confusion came over the woman's face, the arms holding the axe, once more becoming limp.

Susan vomited again.

22

RACE TO BLACK WOOD

"Put your foot down, Dewi." Yvonne placed the flashing light on the dash.

"What if Sheila's just out for an evening walk?"

"Sheila Owen? Out in the sticks? In the dark?" Yvonne pulled a face. "She doesn't have a dog, and I don't see her as the night-owl type. Something's up, I know it is."

"We should wait for backup once we get there." Tasha held onto the handle above her passenger window, stopping herself from being thrown around on the corners. "We don't know what we are facing. We know that the women have used weapons previously. They could have anything out there."

"We can find out the lie of the land once we arrive." Yvonne held the dash to steady herself. "If it looks dangerous, we'll hold back, of course. Backup should arrive soon after we do. It'll be okay."

Tasha sighed. "I wish I had your confidence, Yvonne."

Dewi swung the car into the lay-by, grabbing the torches and other gear from the back. He threw a stab vest each to Yvonne and Tasha. "Get those on," he instructed, before placing one on himself. "I've got my body cam switched on." He handed a torch to Tasha, and took one for himself, fitting his earpiece and radio to his stab vest.

Finally, he handed a taser to Yvonne and fixed another on his belt. "Okay, we're good to go."

They trudged in silence along the lane, allowing the half-moon to light their way, keeping the torch off until they needed to move among the trees.

They were walking for a little over fifteen minutes, when they came to the police cordon surrounding the area where they had discovered the remains of five girls. The place was quiet, save for the occasional hooting of an owl. A quick skim amongst the trees with their torches confirmed the absence of anyone else.

They continued on. They had been walking another fifteen minutes, when the Yvonne stopped and held up her hand to signal the others to be quiet.

As they listened, they could hear voices in the distance, along with grunts and cries. Yvonne led the others in the direction the noises came from.

They bent low, tracking between the trees, approaching a clearing where they could see people in torchlight.

Dewi turned the volume down on his radio.

They crouched at the foot of a large oak, peering round to observe the chaotic scene in the clearing ahead.

"It's Sheila and Pamela. We've got to move, they will kill each other." Yvonne went to get up, but Dewi grabbed her arm.

"Wait, they may not be alone. Get your taser ready."

Pamela lunged at Sheila with the axe. It hit the ground between them, temporarily becoming stuck in the earth. Both women appeared tired and slow.

Yvonne caught sight of Susan Owen seated on the

ground. Susan was talking between gasps for air. "Sheila, Pamela, put the weapons down. You don't want to hurt each other. You want to help each other."

At first, she thought the woman was in control of what was happening between Sheila and Pamela, who were still circling. She quickly realised, however, that Susan was a victim, when a figure in dark clothing ran forward to kick the therapist in the midriff.

Susan collapsed, coughing, to a prone position.

"Okay, I'm not waiting any longer, let's go." The DI ran into the clearing shouting to the figure, "Stop! Police!"

Dewi and Tasha followed, Dewi calling to the two women, "Police! Put down your weapons!"

They were oblivious. Sheila lunged at Pamela with the knife.

Yvonne tasered Sheila Winters while Dewi tasered Pamela Mercer. They did so for the women's own safety. Sheila and Pamela fell to the ground, their bodies twitching.

Tasha ran to Susan Owen. "Susan? Susan, can you hear me?" It was then she caught sight of the dark shape taking off through the trees. "Through there," Tasha shouted, pointing to the direction the figure had gone.

Yvonne and Dewi checked their taser victims' breathing and pulses.

Tasha lay Susan in the recovery position and set off after the dark figure.

"Tasha!" Yvonne left Dewi with the three women and set off after the psychologist.

Shouts went up from the edge of the wood. Backup had arrived.

A myriad torches pierced the gloom, getting closer.

Police dogs barked in the distance.

Yvonne could see Tasha ahead. The psychologist had

slowed, flicking her head left to right, as she searched the trees and undergrowth with her torch.

Her heart thudding in her chest, the DI ran as fast and as quietly as she could to catch up.

"What do you think you're doing?" She whispered to Tasha between gasps for breath.

"He's here somewhere," Tasha whispered back. "He's gone to ground."

They could hear the dogs and the noise of the police team coming up behind.

The figure made a run for it.

Yvonne set off after him, quickly followed by Tasha.

Avoiding tripping over a gnarled tree root, the DI was within six feet of the fugitive, when she dived for his ankles, catching his back one while he was mid-pace.

He fell face-down in the dirt, howling as he went.

Tasha dived on top of him, holding him down, while Yvonne scrambled for her rigid cuffs.

It took a minute for the two of them to subdue him enough to cuff him from behind.

The DI flipped him over. "Simon Hopkins." She grimaced, pulling him into a seated position, just as the first of the backup officers arrived. "Simon Hopkins, I am arresting you on suspicion of kidnapping and incitement to murder." She read him his rights.

"Why not murder?" Tasha asked, as uniformed officers led him away.

"We don't have enough for a direct charge of murder, though that may change. The CPS may decide that he *is* directly responsible for the murder of the five girls and, if they do, we can charge him accordingly."

∼

THEY HOISTED Susan Owen into the ambulance, wearing an oxygen mask, after paramedics had carried out emergency work on a suspected punctured left lung.

Yvonne squeezed her hand. "I'll come and see you tomorrow," she called to her before the back doors were closed.

Tasha rubbed Yvonne's arm. "Are you okay?"

Yvonne nodded. "She was one brave woman out there, risking her life like that."

"She was."

"And so were you." The DI turned to Tasha, taking her into her arms. "What did you think you were doing, putting yourself in harm's way like that? You're not a trained officer, I don't expect you to go after a dangerous suspect on your own. You scared me half to death."

"Were you worried?" Tasha grinned.

Yvonne pulled a face. "It terrified me. I don't know what I would do if I lost you. You're my world. I haven't forgotten the time, a few years ago, when the Priest Killer kidnapped you. I don't want to see anything like that happen again. I love you."

"I love you, too, and I love it when you get all protective over me." Tasha pressed a kiss to the DI's lips. "The statements can wait until tomorrow. Let's go home."

RECOVERY

They had propped Susan up with pillows in her hospital bed as she watched news reports of the night's events in Black Wood. She winced at the DI. "They're making me out to be some sort of heroine," she said, holding her side.

Yvonne placed a punnet of grapes and a magazine on the bedside cabinet, before taking a seat next to the hypnotherapist. "You are a heroine." She took hold of Sheila's hand, careful not to disturb the cannula taped to the back of it. "What you did out there was incredibly brave. I don't condone it. You should have called me with your suspicions about a colleague. He could have killed you. As it is, you've ended up here, a little worse for wear."

"I would have called you." Susan sighed. "It's just that I wasn't sure."

"Did you know it was Simon Hopkins, when you set off?"

"I couldn't be certain it was him, but he was the one sitting next to me at the dinner we attended, and he was the one I talked to about Sheila's recall. I thought he listened intently. Now, I know why."

"How did you know they would be in the wood last night?"

"I received a text from Pamela Mercer on an unknown mobile number. She thanked me for my help and said she wanted to see the dead girls. At first, I didn't understand. Then, I realised what she meant. I tried texting her back, but her phone was out of signal. My intuition told me it was Black Wood."

"She must have texted you on Sheila's mobile. Did you guess the danger you were walking into?"

Susan shook her head. "I didn't. I thought Pamela might have had pangs of conscience about killing the girl, and I thought she was heading there to apologise at the gravesite. I thought she might harm herself. I intended comforting her and bring her back. Help her adjust. I would have gotten her home and called you."

"Why didn't you call me after she texted you?"

"I wasn't confident enough in my suspicions. I thought I would see if I was right, first. I honestly did not know Sheila would be there, much less that they would try to kill each other, driven on by a criminal therapist. I had no idea I'd be walking into that."

"You know you saved those women's lives, don't you? They likely would have killed or severely injured each other before we arrived, if you hadn't intervened."

"I should have called you the minute I suspected Pamela of heading to Black Wood. I'll know next time."

Yvonne grimaced. "Let's hope there is never a next time. I wonder how Sheila and Pamela are feeling?"

Susan leaned her head back against her pillows. "They won't remember much of the events. It is possible, they won't remember anything. They were in a trance. They may know something took place, but they likely won't be able to give you details. They were not responsible for anything that happened."

The DI nodded. "I know, thank you for reminding me."

"I would like to thank you, too, Inspector?"

"Please, call me Yvonne. Why do you want to thank *me*?"

"You saved my life and, actually, you saved the other women's lives, too. I was out of action by the time you got there. I could see they were continuing the fight, but I was running out of air. I could no longer talk them out of it."

"We did a good job, collectively." Yvonne nodded. "Anyway, I hope you like grapes and I brought you the TV Times. Looks like you may be here for a while, and you'll want to know what's on the box or the radio."

Susan grinned. "Thank you, Yvonne."

The DI rose, squeezing the therapist's hand again. "You rest up, now. Get well soon. I've got a killer to charge."

Susan smiled. "Go get him, Inspector."

THE HOSPITAL DISCHARGED Pamela and Sheila with minor injuries.

The DI had given them a day to settle, and for mental health workers to assess them both before she interviewed them. Not that they could remember much, she knew that, but anything they could recall would form part of the evidence against Hopkins.

"A jury may take some convincing, you know, when this goes to trial." Dewi popped his statements next to the DI.

"Of what?" Yvonne asked, prising her eyes from her paperwork.

"Of hypnotherapy being so powerful it could make women hurt others and not remember doing it for decades."

The DI tilted her head, her eyes narrowed. "Perhaps, but that's only because hypnosis is a such a mysterious and unknown entity to the world at large. I am sure we'll have enough experts in place that we can convince the jury of its efficacy."

Dewi ran a hand through his hair. "Well, now I know that it's not something to mess with."

"It can have amazing benefits in the correct hands."

"In the correct hands, being the crucial point."

Yvonne grinned. "You're right, Dewi. Now, are you feeling sleepy?"

"Why?"

The DI deepened her voice in an exaggerated imitation of a hypnotist. "You want to make a round of tea..."

Her DS pouted, placing his hands on his hips. "If I were you, I would ask for your money back from comedy school."

THE END

AFTERWORD

Mailing list: You can join my emailing list here : Annamarie Morgan.com

Facebook page: AnnamarieMorganAuthor

You might also like to read the other books in the series:
   Book 1: Death Master:
   After months of mental and physical therapy, Yvonne Giles, an Oxford DI, is back at work and that's just how she likes it. So when she's asked to hunt the serial killer responsible for taking apart young women, the DI jumps at the chance but hides the fact she is suffering debilitating flashbacks. She is told to work with Tasha Phillips, an in-her-face, criminal psychologist. The DI is not enamoured with the idea. Tasha has a lot to prove. Yvonne has a lot to get over. A tentative link with a 20 year-old cold case brings them closer to the truth but events then take a horrifyingly personal turn.

Book 2: You Will Die

After apprehending an Oxford Serial Killer, and almost losing her life in the process, DI Yvonne Giles has left England for a quieter life in rural Wales.Her peace is shattered when she is asked to hunt a priest-killing psychopath, who taunts the police with messages inscribed on the corpses.Yvonne requests the help of Dr. Tasha Phillips, a psychologist and friend, to aid in the hunt. But the killer is one step ahead and the ultimatum, he sets them, could leave everyone devastated.

Book 3: Total Wipeout

A whole family is wiped out with a shotgun. At first glance, it's an open-and-shut case. The dad did it, then killed himself. The deaths follow at least two similar family wipeouts – attributed to the financial crash.

So why doesn't that sit right with Detective Inspector Yvonne Giles? And why has a rape occurred in the area, in the weeks preceding each family's demise? Her seniors do not believe there are questions to answer. DI Giles must therefore risk everything, in a high-stakes investigation ofa mysterious masonic ring and players in high finance.

Can she find the answers, before the next innocent family is wiped out?

Book 4: Deep Cut

In a tiny hamlet in North Wales, a female recruit is murdered whilst on Christmas home leave. Detective Inspector Yvonne Giles is asked to cut short her own leave, to investigate. Why was the young soldier killed? And is her death related to several alleged suicides at her army base? DI Giles this it is, and that someone powerful has a dark secret they will do anything to hide.

Book 5: The Pusher

Young men are turning up dead on the banks of the River Severn. Some of them have been missing for days or even weeks. The only thing the police can be sure of, is that the men have drowned. Rumours abound that a mythical serial killer has turned his attention from the Manchester canal to the waterways of Mid-Wales. And now one of CID's own is missing. A brand new recruit with everything to live for. DI Giles must find him before it's too late.

Book 6: Gone

Children are going missing. They are not heard from again until sinister requests for cryptocurrency go viral. The public must pay or the children die. For lead detective Yvonne Giles, the case is complicated enough. And then the unthinkable happens...

Book 7: Bone Dancer

A serial killer is murdering women, threading their bones back together, and leaving them for police to find. Detective Inspector Yvonne Giles must find him before more innocent victims die. Problem is, the killer wants her and will do anything he can to get her. Unaware that she, herself, is is a target, DI Giles risks everything to catch him.

Book 8: Blood Lost

A young man comes home to find his whole family missing. Half-eaten breakfasts and blood spatter on the lounge wall are the only clues to what happened...

Book 9: Angel of Death

He is watching. Biding his time. Preparing himself for a

torturous kill. *Soaring above; lord of all. His journey, direct through the lives of the unsuspecting.*

The Angel of Death is nigh.

The peace of the Mid-Wales countryside is shattered, when a female eco-warrior is found crucified in a public wood. At first, it would appear a simple case of finding which of the woman's enemies had had her killed. But DI Yvonne Giles has no idea how bad things are going to get. As the body count rises, she will need all of her instincts, and the skills of those closest to her, to stop the murderous rampage of the Angel of Death.

Book 10: Death in the Air

Several fatal air collisions have occurred within a few months in rural Wales. According to the local Air Accidents Investigation Branch (AAIB) inspector, it's a coincidence. Clusters happen. Except, this cluster is different. DI Yvonne Giles suspects it when she hears some of the witness statements but, when an AAIB inspector is found dead under a bridge, she knows it.

Something is way off. Yvonne is determined to get to the bottom of the mystery, but exactly how far down the treacherous rabbit hole is she prepared to go?

Book 11: Death in the Mist

The morning after a viscous sea-mist covers the seaside town of Aberystwyth, a young student lies brutalised within one hundred yards of the castle ruins.

DI Yvonne Giles' reputation precedes her. Having successfully captured more serial killers than some detectives have caught colds, she is seconded to head the murder investigation team, and hunt down the young woman's killer.

What she doesn't know, is this is only the beginning...

Remember to watch out for Book 13, coming soon...

Printed in Poland
by Amazon Fulfillment
Poland Sp. z o.o., Wrocław

55887904R00101